THREE
POEMS

ALSO BY MICHAEL McCLURE

POETRY
Hymns to Saint Geryon
Dark Brown
The New Book / A Book of
    Torture
Ghost Tantras
Little Odes
Organism
Star
September Blackberries
Rare Angel
Jaguar Skies
Antechamber
Fragments of Perseus
Selected Poems
Rebel Lions
Simple Eyes

NOVELS
The Mad Cub
The Adept

PLAYS
The Blossom
The Mammals
The Beard
Gargoyle Cartoons
The Grabbing of the Fairy

Gorf
General Gorgeous
Josephine the Mouse Singer
VKTMS

ESSAYS
Meat Science Essays
Scratching the Beat Surface
Specks
Testa Coda
Lighting the Corners

COLLABORATIVE
"Mercedes Benz," with Janis
    Joplin
Mandala Book, with Bruce
    Conner
Freewheelin Frank, Secretary of
    the Angels: As Told to
    Michael McClure, by Frank
    Reynolds

CD, VIDEO, AND
    CASSETTE
Love Lion, video, with Ray
    Manzarek
Love Lion, CD, with Ray
    Manzarek
Ghost Tantras, audio cassette

MICHAEL McCLURE

Introduction by Robert Hunter

THREE
POEMS

3

Dolphin Skull, Rare Angel, and Dark Brown

PENGUIN POETS

PENGUIN BOOKS
Published by the Penguin Group
Penguin Books USA Inc., 375 Hudson Street, New York, New York 10014, U.S.A.
Penguin Books Ltd, 27 Wrights Lane, London W8 5TZ, England
Penguin Books Australia Ltd, Ringwood, Victoria, Australia
Penguin Books Canada Ltd, 10 Alcorn Avenue,
Toronto, Ontario, Canada M4V 3B2
Penguin Books (N.Z.) Ltd, 182–190 Wairau Road,
Auckland 10, New Zealand

Penguin Books Ltd, Registered Offices:
Harmondsworth, Middlesex, England

First published in Penguin Books 1995

10 9 8 7 6 5 4 3 2 1

Dark Brown was originally published by The Auerhahn Press, 1961,
and later in a volume with *Hymns to St. Geryon* by Grey Fox Press, 1967.
Rare Angel was first published by Black Sparrow Press, 1974.

Library of Congress Cataloging-in-Publication Data
McClure, Michael.
    [Poems. Selections]
    Three poems / Michael McClure ; foreword by Robert Hunter.
      p.   cm.
    Contents: Dolphin skull—Rare angel—Dark brown.
    ISBN 0 14 058.709 8
    I. Title.
   PS3563.A262T55   1995
   811'.54—dc20   94-47326

Printed in the United States of America
Set in Electra
Designed by Katy Riegel

Once this was all Black Plasma
and Imagination

INTRODUCTION

Right understanding of late twentieth century poetics can be impeded by use of critical tools of other times. *Direction* is more often to the point.

Though Michael McClure's images do double service as symbols, he is not a symbolist. His objects are clear and present, things in themselves, not a referral service for ideal forms. That they express the world of the ideal is rather an inevitable side effect of rigorous objectivity. The work is endowed with emotion and morality and a decidedly anarcho-leftist politic, but these features are largely exterior to a more specific aim, a purely poetic gesture.

Though McClure's poetry is neither programmatic nor perversely exclusive of meaning it is needful to grasp what he's trying to achieve in order to realize how well he has succeeded. The key is this: he does not make things up. He reports with exactness. Fastidious exactness.

This may seem an odd estimation when his lines routinely exhibit the hyper clarity and thronging of image peculiar to hallucination, but his trademark rhapsody is the natural dance of clearly observed items. Fantasy is minimal, though the sensations and types of imagery associated with it are everywhere present.

Fantasy is the imagination of the imagination; the envisionings of abstracted vision. The phenomenological iota is set aside in favor of associative chains which recede further and further from the conditioning image. It is essentially the troping of trope leading to dream territory; an engrossing and sometimes powerful mode of poetic procedure but *not* McClure's territory. Not to denigrate the fantastical approach here, simply to delineate the realm of the surreal and differentiate its effects from McClure's area of primary concern.

Although a certain surface sensuality gives itself easily enough, it is impossible to read McClure's work quickly at depth. Time must be taken to envision what is indicated, to link visions with the poet. Reading his words without making an effort to engage their visual and visceral potential is an exercise in page turning; a postcard in place of a sunset.

Appreciating the long-term presence of a theoretic bias grounded in specific objectivizing technique is crucial in apprehending the essentials of McClure's poetry. It is his poetic faith, one that locates him alongside elders William Carlos Williams and Charles Olson in the canon of Projective Verse.

Neither a word collagist, nor one who allows himself to be much influenced by the suggestive directions words tempt a poet to take by virtue of their customary associative potentials (most prominently in rhyme), McClure firmly guides words to report objects of experience, however visionary these objects may be. If, as sometimes happens, his subject matter is precisely the evocative power of a particular word, such as *aelf*, a similar approach is employed. Unlike more austere practitioners of the Projective form, he makes little attempt to remove himself from the equation, recognizing the viewer to be as much a part of the skyscape as the clouds.

While adhering to the Projective canon, McClure's conceptual forte is grounded in an informed Zen mode of perception, focused at ease within the moment. His other purely stylistic concern is the specific attention to breath groups in spoken poetry characteristic of the Beat movement, of which predilection he is a recognized germinal feature.

McClure professes and employs Projective method primarily to report movements of what can only be called primordial ecstasy in the life of the biological organism, the visions of its biologic mind, and its essential animal spirit. That this requires a sensation of at-oneness with the subject matter is not surprising. Spiritual precision, if that is not a self-cancelling description, is his specialty, and it may be that no poet does this particular thing better, employing the technique, as he has, throughout the better part of his lengthy career. His work, to be seen aright, must be viewed through that lens; his relative success and failure judged by reference to how closely a particular poem approximates his avowed intention.

If it may be maintained that a *true* reporting is an act of poetic perfection, hence completion—if perfectly referential and adequately represented in words—it would follow that McClure's work is perfectly complete at any moment, insofar and just so far as he is true to his method, and this seems to be the case. The work does not progress towards some distant apex of excellence. It simply inhabits that excellence and accumulates. It is instructive to see the subjective changes wrought by long experience upon the projectively perceived object, but the castle is already captured and only the itemization of its contents remains to be completed. Poetic Reality is at work here, that rare angel most convincingly summoned by being true to a worthy idea for a very long period of time.

Reportage is the key in appreciating McClure. Should spots of red fruit appear squashed on a white cupboard, the image is one actually experienced. You can trust McClure for that. The spots were not yellow. It is good to know this.

—Robert Hunter

CONTENTS

AUTHOR'S PREFACE

There are three lives here in one book: *Dolphin Skull, Rare Angel,* and *Dark Brown.* Each is like a living being with eyes and ears and fingers, and each is as different from one another as living creatures are unique. I wrote all three spontaneously in Projective Verse, using the syllable and the energy of the breath as the structure of the poem.

To write spontaneously does not mean to write carelessly or without thought and deep experience. In fact, there must be a vision and a poetics that are alive and conscious.

The moment of writing is complex and at the same time it is natural and vigorous. I do not know of a more adventurous gesture than to write spontaneously. Whether a poem is born from exuberance or depression, there must be ebullience, hunger for freedom, and imagination. When the poem is finished I listen to it and look at it on the screen or in the ink of the pen, and see that it has a deeper consciousness and brighter thoughts than I was aware of while writing. Sometimes there is difficulty in a poem. The obscurity, the ununderstandability, is not there for the purpose of evasion, but it is the energy compressing and leaping and rippling, just as a wave ripples with silver in the moonlight. Even in darkness one can see that it is a silver wave. Goethe believed that poetry should be incomprehensible and incommensurable. All art is that way to some degree, but much art seems flat and lacking in courage because it neglects to be difficult.

If poetry and science cannot change one's life they are meaningless. The meaning is that we may become more able to ring true to our deep selves. If a poet risks being accused of esotericism in order to be vigorous and to give meaning to the poem, then that's a small price.

What is urgent is not the *quantity* that is understood as one reads a poem, but how much one uses the richness of one's being to have the experience of the poem.

Dark Brown was written when I was a young man and I used poetry to revolt against society during the fifties Cold War, but equally as important was to rebel against my own customs and habits. It was a dark night of the soul, and I wanted to use liberational methods to discover the substance of spirit. I believed that spirit was one and the same as the body. My intention was to discover the true shape of spirit and love, and I found I had to invent them: they were not there unless I created them. After the first stanzas of *Dark Brown* were written, a word vision occurred as "Fuck Ode," and then, beyond that, I was surprised by the last section of the poem, "A Garland." How can a young man search for his body and not come to speak of sexuality?

Dark Brown is about the biological roots of the impulse to freedom and how that struggle relates to poetry, and it is about setting language free from censorship. My earliest essay, "Phi Upsilon Kappa," is about writing *Dark Brown*, and another essay, "Revolt," is about the biology of it; both could be used as notes for the poem (both essays appear in the collection *Meat Science Essays*). To bring light to my dark cloud I followed renegade paths and also immersed myself in scholarship. *Dark Brown* contains words from Old English and dictionaries of archaisms and argot. This was a search for language to describe the states for which I could not find contemporary words. Moreover, I was looking at natural history and trying to understand the principles that join living organisms together in simple and complex structures. Not knowing where I was, except for my presence there, I studied the physics that was complementary to my state, and found it in the ideas of Wolfgang

Pauli and P.A.M. Dirac. My novel, *The Mad Cub*, describes some of the personal life behind the poem.

In beginning *Rare Angel*, the second poem of *Three Poems*, I determined to write directly from sensations of my body. But preceding the writing there was much studying and traveling with friends who showed me Nature and the environment. I was fascinated by Whitehead's thoughts on Reason and by the physics of Hwa Yen Buddhism. *Rare Angel* is motivated by some of the same impulses as *Dark Brown*, and it strives, like our bodies, to be in the present, the past, and the future simultaneously—in the "uncarved block" of the Taoists. Some of the experiences in *Rare Angel* are spoken of in *Scratching the Beat Surface* and in *Lighting the Corners*, two books of interviews and prose.

Dolphin Skull is in two sections: "Stanzas in Memory" is written directly from the unconscious in the sense that Jackson Pollock's "psychoanalytic drawings" were from the unconscious—what I saw was simply there and was not planned in order or method except the systemless one that is the creative act. "Portrait of the Moment," the second section, begins with the twelfth stanza of the first section, repeats it, and then continues without interruption to very *consciously* and spontaneously explore that single moment for as long as it unscrolls in sensory images. Consciousness melted my travels through Kenya and Tanzania, when watching eagles and lions and baboons, in with the primal stuff of infancy, youth, manhood, and the present—all in one moment. I see now that all moments are one and the same moment.

Following *Dolphin Skull*, there is an afterword describing the writing of the second section of the poem; it also explains the poem's title.

My gratitude to Dave Haselwood and Andrew Hoyem of Auerhahn Press, who first published *Dark Brown*, and to John and Barbara Martin of Black Sparrow Press, who initially published *Rare Angel*. Further thanks to editor David Stanford, who herein first presents *Dolphin*

Skull, and to the workers at Viking Penguin press who made this book possible. The first public presentation of the opening stanzas of *Dolphin Skull* were with Ray Manzarek playing piano at the Great American Music Hall in San Francisco. The dates on the title pages of the poems represent the year of earliest publication.

My gratitude to photographer Harry Redl for the use of his author portrait on the cover of *Three Poems.*

Thanks to poet/lyricist Robert Hunter for his Introduction and to scholar Harald Mesch for use of our interview. Thanks to all my friends who show me ways to become myself in darkness and light, and to see that the universes are the messiah and the tathagata. Special thanks to my family and to the artists and biologists who lead me, and to Amy Evans who is by my side.

DOLPHIN
SKULL *(1995)*

STANZAS IN MEMORY

The memories of one's youth make for long, long thoughts.
—Lapp proverb

SO THE OWL HOOTS: Turquoise. Musk. White linen.
    Deer in the yard—a stag with antlers.
                                       Boyhood
  in the park of the body that smells like the ocean
  as it washes on the greensward. Your blue eyes.
      YOU. Looking with love. I'll leave you
                              and I ought
  to be scared as my skin wrinkles. The boy dreams
  of Grandpa. As I get huger I become streams
  stretching into shadows of memories. JUST
             AS
             I
         TASTE
       the blackberry,
    as the tiny white flies flurry
      AROUND IT,
  THERE IS THE BLOOD WHERE
    the thorn cuts me. Helicopters
     clatter over the canyon

         IN

          S
          U
          N
          L
          I
          G
          H
          T

Blackness is just a mask of fat for somebody.
The tiny white flies are making a cloud
in the tiers of the brambles
swarming around the dark fruit.
The clouds are alive.
This cloud is a life.

THIS CLOUD IS A LIFE as the great horned owl hoots
three calls.   The pony of memory tramples the rattlesnake.
Sunset colors of apricot and layers of black
over the ocean.   A puff of summer dust where
the buckeye butterfly lands.   Mystic wings
of planets and scarlet nebulae.   A lock
on the machine gun under the bed.
FACES
TWISTED
in
pain
from the old times when love hurt
so much that it is spotlights
filled with legs and mouths
writhing.
Nylon stockings filled with sentimental songs
are stained with blackberry juice like
my fingers.
AND
I
LOVE
YOU,
your blue eyes.
Crinkle of frost on the windows.   This
is all fog off the ocean coming over
the line of brown hills.
TAILGATING
DRIVERS
behind me
with stoic faces
of Arnold Schwarzenegger.
The city is a mammal vision
in peaks of fog.
Jack Pumpkinhead is laughing with the Tin Man
and
an

AXE
chops through it all
showing the dry grain
and the whorls.
Raphael found the rules and was freed.

THE CLOUD THAT RAPHAEL FOUND is the rules of freedom.
Dark green shamrocks grow in a bowl where
dead friends live in dreams.   Sounds of blue-black
jays screaming.   My arm around Robert helping
him into my car.   "Crazy John's new book
is like your poetry," I say, showing him
the fine printing.
"How?" "It's the elegance," I answer.
The gray-brown moth flutters
O
V
E
R
the brick-red and scarlet and blue
of the prayer rug.
YOU,
your blue eyes
the daintiness of your ankle,
your deep wit,
these are the reasons I am alive.
Miró knows it is all play and Pollock understands
the unconscious power.

NOW

THERE

ARE

LIONS

IN

THE

WOODWORK.

Now I smell my Grandma as she looks
at me through her thick glasses.
Now I understand the sexual addiction
of my young manhood
was a CRUCIFIXION—
glittering and lovely
AS
an ostrich boa and smashed mirrors

seen on acid.

Eagles seen on acid are the rules
that are broken in old poetry.   The fierce eye,
the naying hand of the boy.   The cracks
                                        with festoons
of dust on the yellowing plaster ceiling.   Broken
old car doors tied shut with ropes.   Please come
and take care of me, is the child's prayer
grimly pleaded
into a black
eternity
becoming the bulk
of
the body.

          MY
          GOD   MY GOD!

          NO   MY GOD!

          don't   MY GOD!

          DO
          THIS

          to me!

DON'T DO THIS TO ME!
DON'T DO THIS TO ME!
DON'T DO THIS TO ME!
I am alone in Grandpa's dark basement
praying to you.
I don't want to become an eagle
when I die!
Don't let the flames burst from this sooty smoke!
There is the endless concrete freeway in the sun
—then the cool fog.

I
HAVE
BLOWN UP!
Blown up and cooked myself over a fire.
Smell the pot roast and the noodles.   I can
hear my eardrums burst.
Toes on damp moss.   Broken shells in sand.

BʀOKEN SHELLS IN SAND are not superhuman.
Everything is divine.
The body is the soul.   The intelligent body.   Cries
from the sand are little crabs' eyes.   Creepy and bright and
the musky smell of decaying algae in sunshine.
A cold wind makes chilblains and bumps on the skin.
Going back to the moment of the big bang.
The big bang is the consciousness of lions dispersing
the eagles.   An eagle lands on the bare tree
by the car and tears up a rabbit. Souls are
dead babies.
YOU
know these things
like the smell of new tires
—while flight after flight of planes
with bombs pass over.   I
AM
STILL
here, just as I ever was.
I am furious and fragile and trembling.
JUST
AS
I
ever was.
BEGGING
is heroic.   Striding
as free
as spirit
can in
its swirls.
Breaking up rainbows of agonies into actions.
Part of this dark flow
that is
turned over and over by the hands of light
with fingernails of movies.
MOVIES OF SUNS

spraying
the darkness.
Gray hair on the floor.

GRAY hair on the floor and the radio talking.
STEERING WHEEL
more real than anything else.   Foggy yellow lights
in the tunnel.
Skinny, addled, wrinkled, childlike, old Horowitz playing
SCRIABIN

on

TV.
Me, playing this beautiful pen.

MORE

ALIVE

THAN

I

OUGHT

TO

BE.

More alive than I ought to be.
Oceans and freeways of grief and guilt.
Triumphs of bare feet and drugs up the nose.
Child of cocaine and raccoons in hollow logs.
"φύσις κρύπτεσθαι φιλει"
Nature loves to hide herself
in
Leonardo's
secret
language
and the dimensions that disappeared
after the bang.

OLD
MEN
DREAMING
OF
GREAT-GRANDFATHERS
ARE
VERY
WISE
like sow bugs
and wooden spools wound
with scarlet thread
and an antlered buck that drinks
from a bowl in the yard
in moonshadows.

THE SOW BUG RESTS in the shadow of a pine cone
and red cars
cruise by while the world
is making itself with my senses.
Can this be the beginning of old age?
Fear comes in stars of consciousness
and
NOW
I
AM
somewhere else.
The thorns in my finger make stars.
The blackberry is sweet and black
and red and bitter.
Cries of redtail hawks are imitated by blue-black jays.
COVERS
OF OLD MAGAZINES
are glossy, erotic, my
sexuality
grows underneath them
like a rock rolled up on a beach
by the edge of huge waves.
I'M
LISTENING
to you in my mind.
A MUSEUM OF DIRTY PICTURES.
NO
ONE
IS
INTERESTED
BUT
the lion knows as he speaks
to the eagle.   This is all BLACKNESS,
this is a cave holding a bowl of beef soup
with the leaves and odors of Vietnamese basil.

I
WILL
NOT EAT BABY ANIMALS!
TO CHEW ON THEIR RIBS IS TASTY AND REVOLTING.
I am spirit.   I am a child with you.

SPIRIT, I AM A CHILD WITH YOU.   Everything is an homage
to Jack Kerouac while Norman Mailer creates
great
EXISTENTIAL
ACTS
larger than literature.
Larger than literature entering through the realm
of the senses
—what is called the *sensorium.*
Brown baboon turning around on the log
to look at us.
Inventing lives.
Running fingers through the clinks
of smooth rocks.
In rage, pushing a friend into the swimming pool
near the pygmy mongooses.   Elephant skeletons
spread out like explosions
on
the
dry
yellow
grass
—and gyrfalcons
squawking with anger
flying round their nest
in the cliff.
The car tries to drive over me from behind
like my stepfather's face.
AND
WHAT
TRIUMPHS
of sexuality and pride
LIKE BABY LAMBS
cavorting and happily and clumsily
butting old wooden fences
in the darkness

[17]

OF

CARNIVORE

CONSCIOUSNESS.

Stick figures of Jack and Jill.

STICK FIGURES OF JACK AND JILL.   Figures of Jack and Jill
and the teacher's face like a huge moth in midair.
Billy Goats Gruff look at the pattern
on the wings.   Red and brown
planets with auras and the miraculous pitcher.
Crayfish in ponds under bridges.
A dead friend's eyes through
his wire-rim glasses.
His laugh has become part of my bones.
THIS
CITY
OF
MY HEART
was once innocent as a baby and we
grew up in it. Shoe shops.   Bakeries.   Umbrella shops
in department stores.
Seasons of heavy rains and babies.   Cold silver
wings.   Steaming food on a wooden table.
EX
TREMES
OF
POVERTY.
Agonies over the rent.
FACES
TWISTED

BY

LOVE

IN

THE
NIGHT.
BODIES
tearing

at
one
another
like sleek figures
high
on the drugs of our glands.
And still we are all gods and I have a huge face.

I AM A GOD WITH A HUGE FACE.   Lions
and eagles pour out of my mouth.   Big white
square teeth and a red-purple tongue.   There are
magenta clouds around my head and this
is my throne room.   Actors perform
the drama of my being inside of you,
WEARING
YOUR
SKIN.
I
am
writhing and clawing.
BEG FOR MERCY.
Blackberry bramble catching
my pants leg.   A tearing sound.
Deep inside in the padded car.
Garbage truck full of petroleum fantasies.
Dogs barking under the dark
tall pine trees.   Hollyhocks
and a few pink roses.   You are
everyone
BUT
I am nobody.
Nobody is very large
and
powerful.
Memory is naked bodies
in a battle.   The war is sensuous
as a little boy's penis.
Fighter planes are guns.
I am the river god
in love with my dreams.
Not dreams but ongoing presences
spewed from the bang
through a nervous system.

At the edge of things but reaching
way back inside.

WAY BACK INSIDE is the castle of things.
These things never were except as I knew them.
A white polar bear rug on a shining floor.
Glass eyes and huge yellow teeth.   Fossil ivory.
Christmas trees with tinsel.   A friend
blown up in a car wreck.   False voices
of self assurance.   Peyote visions
like endless counters at Kresses.   Shoe polish
lids.   Shoe polish lids and lint.   Brooms
with dark grease on them.
The view of the brown hills by moonlight
while the crickets sing.   The sound
of rocks as they move in the river
and a moldy deer skeleton with ribs
ripped out by the jaws of the cougar.
THIS
IS
ALL
ME
the same as I ever was,
crying in movies, LAUGHING
and drunk and kicking
a door in with long hair
blown back
in
the wind
of my hormones.
Sneaky and Proud.
W
A
T
C
H
I
N
G

the fire while mysterious
beings form in the air.
Faust wants no more.
Never say: Hold, let this moment never cease.

HOLD, LET THIS MOMENT never cease.   Drag it out
of context look at the roots of it in quarks
and primal hydrogen.   It's the sound
of Shelley's laugh in my ears.
YOU
THINK
WE
ARE
BODIES
WALKING
UP   Kissing.
TO   Holding hands.
ONE
ANOTHER
AND
SPEAKING.
A universe before man ever was, filled
with dragonflies
in
your
eardrums.
Palm trees and skyscrapers.   Vervet monkey
in the euphorbia tree staring at me.
The lion is consciousness.   The eagle
is experience.   As real as mud
chiming
with light
from
rainbows.
"Fuck you," right in your face.
"Fuck you!" He pulls out a gun
in reply.   Gun the size of a toilet.
Blue-black.   Bullets fire into a world
made of stacks of dirty feet.
Eyes of starving families.   Dust
from red clay.   Something

[25]

is purring
or flying.
Sound of thunder jars loose dead leaves
and they slowly fall
while the bell rings.

THERE IS NO CONFLICT IN MEMORY while the bell rings.
Free association is a red-blue tongue
up the ass.   She looks like
Elizabeth Taylor.   It's a penthouse
and the mind is there and somewhere else.
Robert Duncan called these things
G
L
A
M
O
U
R
S.
"Mind" means nothing but consciousness—
a rock has it and a toadstool
and a field of subparticles in a complex protein
as it loops, tying a knot.   A mouth
with a cock in it.   Babies
crying in the next room.   Blackberries
glisten with it and the webs covered
with dust and particles from car fumes
and the pollen of eucalyptus.
Sometimes there is the sound
of attack
rifles

and
the
AM
TRAK

between owl hoots.   Turquoise.
Musk.   White linen.   Pelican ink.
Concrete walls with words
on

them
in spotlights.
Ride a cock horse to Banbury Cross
where an old toad hops in the basement
in the smell of blueing.

WATER BOILS IN THE BIG COPPER TUB. White sheets
will be dipped in the blueing. Wrung out in the wringer
and then hung up to dry. THE SUBSTRATE IS SO VIBRANT
that I can't get close to it. It is YOU. YOU who are
as the owl hoots. Van Gogh drawing
must have felt like this. The hunter
throwing the chipped stone hand axe. Flint
and obsidian. A spirit rises from blood.
THE SUBSTRATE IS SO VIOLENT.
VOLATILE.
VIBRANT
I
birth
myself
in memories
just as Böhme's vision of dawn.
AND
YOU
CRAWL
from the gold,
liquid gold of rosy color
and
give birth to me.
You are my memories of you
holding my hand.
I
WANT
TO
GO
ANYWHERE.
I am a flowering.
Brave. Fearful. Scared to death
by the boredom. A fat gray kitten rolling
on its back, sinking its baby claws
(clean, thin, baby claws)

into a soft pink hand.
That's all, *fin*.   *Finis*.   The end
of beginning.   The old rabbit winks.

THE OLD RABBIT BEGINS TO WINK, then the pony
tramples the rattlesnake.   Eagle bones in a dream.
The eternal dimensions before the bang
have closed themselves off.   This one
tries to be the realm of entropy.
Sombreros the color of children's
cookies.   Colorlessness at the edges
of things.   Radiances of blue-silver
clouds and mountain ranges
of cool white fog.   I'm in a black suit
with wide legs.   You.   You are elegant
with soft arms
and strong fingers.

THERE

IS

JOY

IN

THE

ROOM

sometimes and
it is the field of complex
presences.

Big clear laughs are the best
and deep seeing eyes
looking back through the muscles
of mastodon hunters
out

towards
the edge of the solar system
and a wall of surprising stars.
All of this through the background
BLUR
of one-dimensionality,
psyche projections,
and vibrancies of the substrate
as it turns
itself inside-out like a protein.

INSIDE-OUT LIKE A PROTEIN the owl hoots.
Big trouble.   A child is waiting.   Love streams.
Learn indolence from dust.   Tonto says, owl hoots
are people in ambush.   Incommensurable
and incomprehensible are the best of poetic creation,
the old man sings.   The galaxies are a river
seen from this direction.   The child knows
it is all black behind the eyes
and that flesh is a swirl of hungry
fantasies,
each loving the other.

M
A
L
L
A
R
M
É

throws it down on the deck
of the sinking ship in the storm
and the maelstrom.
SNAKE EYES!
Right on the planks!
Skeletons bartering their muscles
for gold.
Not likely
but the glitter is divine as the caterpillar.

I
HATED
HATED
HATED
the bombers flying over.
I could not save them or myself.
Napalm.   The demon self

with soft eyes.   Stabbing
Hamlet in the throne room.   Discover
you are Hamlet with the blade
up your ass.

YOU ARE HAMLET WITH A BLADE OF GRASS
in your teeth like an old farmer
with a piece of straw.   Cracker barrels
where the dog pissed.   This is all a string of pearls
with reflections of reflections in the opulent
glimmering surface of endless flaws
making a surface
for the fingertips to touch
while remembering perfumes.
These are shadows of the wisps
of nothingness.
THIS
IS
A
COLLECTION
of skulls on a mantel: eagle,
lion, bat, goat, raven, sea turtle,
salmon.
A power pack
for the emotions to grow
through the taste of blackberries
and sound of the jays
and the footprints of the stag in the yard.
FREE
as the
cloud
of white flies
in the brambles.   Going
the way of all flesh.
CAUGHT IN THE ROAR OF THE PLANES
PASSING OVER
while the bronze bell rings
in the wind.
Triangles of sunlight pass over the rug,

pretend this is not blackness.
This is not blackness, this
is a bell ring.

PORTRAIT OF THE MOMENT

Sᴛᴏᴘ,

HOLD, LET THIS MOMENT never cease.   Drag it out
    of context, look at the roots of it in quarks
    and primal hydrogen.   It's the sound
    of Shelley's laugh in my ears.
          YOU
          THINK
          WE
          ARE
          BODIES
          WALKING
             UP   Kissing.
             TO   Holding hands.
          ONE
          ANOTHER
          AND
          SPEAKING.
  A universe before man ever was, filled
        with dragonflies
          in
         your
        eardrums.
Palm trees and skyscrapers.   Vervet monkey
in the euphorbia tree staring at me.
    The lion is consciousness.   The eagle
      is experience.   As real as mud
        chiming
        with light
        from
        rainbows.

"Fuck you," right in your face.
"Fuck you!"   He pulls out a gun
in reply. . Gun the size of a toilet.
Blue-black.   Bullets fire into a world
made of stacks of dirty feet.
Eyes of starving families.   Dust
from red clay.   Something
is purring
or flying.
Sound of thunder jars loose dead leaves
and they slowly fall
while the bell rings.
The bell chimes red-headed
linnets
wiping their beaks
on the green lichen.
Planes roar
from the airport
mixing
with sounds
of the traffic.
Raindrops on the brim
of a hat.
Round yellow seeds among hailstones
on the gray wet planks.
The self coming out like CLOUD,
CLOUD of FACES
and shoulders.
Big cloud.   Bulk.   Made
out of meat.   All imagin-
ation like the river god, rippling
shoulders and muscles and hungers
and actions and their substrates
in childhood as childhood
has become dark meat like
Rexroth

said.
It's the eagle of experience feathered
with faces.
IT'S THE THOUGHT
OF
THE
BODY
AT
the edge
of
THINGS;
it's
the physics
of physiology,
the universe as athlete.
It's a real *if* like the odor
of chinchilla fur
or car tracks and deer prints
side by side
in
day
old
mud.

REAL

CLOUD

OF
FACES

and gone

now.

Demon warriors and toad men

and sneaky thoughts before glass
   cabinets with secret drawers
and smell of frankincense
   wrapped in pink panties
   and raw meat.   Then buried
in statues of dreams at
    midnight
   by an old barb-
   wire fence.
    While
the car motor
   runs.
The face in each feather
   is dumb and simple.
THE EAGLE AND THE LION ARE RAPT
   IN ONE THING

    BUT

   that is beside the point

   WHERE

   light becomes meat

   BEING

   BURIED

   in boys' leg muscles
   or the plumpness of wrists
and the baby's interlocking
   of eyes.   See ME!
It's ALL at the edge of things
   becoming the matter
    WE

ARE,
making the ground work,
protein groundwork,

from
gases
and stars
in a plasma.   With
all the dimensions there
((IN THAT   ))
we only have hints
of
HERE
in this tiny HUGE space.
Architecture of something else
that is seen as stuff.

AN

INTELLIGENT

FLATWORM

a hammer,
moss rubbed over the surface
of a turquoise,
streetlights in fog,
enzymatic structures of subtle happiness

in
an

OLD
WOMAN'S

WORDS.

Look at her glasses there
     inside of me somewhere
   in the future scratched
     on a scale on a moth's back
next to the vistas of a dark ocean
   seen from the hilltop.
        Children shouting.
"Dog piles" of boy fighting.
Smell of mincemeat pies and snuff.
     Pictures of duck hunting inside
        of sleeping bags.
     Looking down at my solid hands
               posing
        with chunky fingers
of sculpture laid out being themselves
   for me and everybody in an
          IMAGE
     while I look up
   through my dark brows.
As old as what will happen
     and bright as the corners
     of coal bins and the smell
        of coal dust.   Sound of cinders
        dumped out over iron rust.
     AWARENESS ENLARGES.
        A PROCESS
             till
   I walk through caves
        of it.   Wooden
     yoyos.   Alive and lithe
   and powerful as a blue-black
     snake or a wet beach stone,
          IT
        TWISTS
        AND
        WRITHES

with muscles moving
the big scales
I
imagine.   In im-
itation of something
in the original DARK
DENSITY
that never was till
this place

O
N

T
H
E

S
C
R
O
L
L

with the chunky fingers
laid out over themselves
and my eyes looking
up through dark brows.

WHAT POWER!
What power if power is
luminosity and darkness
in patinated bronze
like a bell ring.

Lines of tigers and owls

in glyphs speaking of ceremonies
turned bluegreen, patchy
dark greenblack and crusty brown,
smooth as the surface of a tooth.
Everything taken from damp tombs.
Sexuality is there:
A
CRAMP
in the neck and shoulders
STOPPING
the smooth flowery pleasure from
rippling through the somatic
segments.
Making a tilt to the head,
an engaging look,
in its formation
coming up out of baby meat
as a gloss on both sides
of the scroll.   The scroll
is the point that is never there.
Kicking down a door and shouting
in drunken rage, long hair
blown back with storm of hormones.
Paper-mâché Santa Clauses
brought out in the smell
of unwrapped Gouda cheese
with scent of lizard
excrement on the fingers
and
stacks
of comic books
like folklore riffling
images of Puck and Pookah
and comic caped creatures
with goggles diving
from windows

IN
ALL
THE
DEEP,
DEEP
THOUGHT

of dimensions seeking
to return to their full complexity.
Everywhere in drafts and rainbows,
  dusty windowshades and screaming murders.
Night sounds of cities on Easter morning.
All of the outside swirled in the instant,
  its cytoplasm and mitochondrial
  stars as building blocks for the rooms
    we inhabit.   Never put the finger
  on it.   The sun reflected on dull nails.
HOLD, this must not cease.   Her jasmine
odor on the stone bridge over the river.
      Fear I am losing her.   Red-brown
  cowboy boots.   Heel sounds on cobblestone
    in darkness.   Harmonica playing while
      the robins sing.   There's no surprises
here.   We are all always here.   THIS
                IS
          PHILOSOPHY
              OF
          WHITEHEAD'S
              PRE
          HENSION.
Hysterical Socrates at the window
    giggling   Dried roses standing
    in the dusty vinegar cruet
  making energy for an old poem.   Passion
    in the chest is beating like blood
      and the singular intelligence of a mammal

in an old soft shirt and Levi's.   It's all
passion and calmness.   Meat and air.   Tendrils.
Tendrils growing from tendrils, lashing out
of tendrils interwinding and twining
in the primal stuff of the future
where there used to be sunlight through
the window
on the wooden furniture
as I look up through dark brows
throwing light on the camera there.
Rimbaud guessed it and Artaud
is a brother in the dusty basement
with dirt under feet and a flashlight
looking for heroin as I clutch
Mickey Mouse and Goofy, spinning
through sexy corridors
of unread books.   The tunnel is the outside
and matter is a dot of nothing on no
scroll.   Not even
a
gloss.   The passion
is real.   (The eagle,
the lion.   The tiger, the wolf.)
Passion remains when the matter
disappears.   It is comprised
of the absence of the absence of nothingness.
Passion is the chest and the wrists
and the elbows in the moment.
All moments are one deep density
as garbage trucks are and a plane
passing over.   The white bell blossoms
of the naked-branched manzanita
say it in the raindrops.   The regret
and the guilt are bursting inside
with fleshly joy and torn
scraps of blue plastic paper

on the moving roller.   Where the twin
fawns may starve together
in a vision of the goddess of Mercy
and

GRAVITY
WAVES

are
hallucinations
caused by the absence
of senses.   The sensorium
is unlimited but it is out of touch
with the density Dimensions.
This is a prow cutting through
it
all,
being it all as
I slip out into it

WHERE IT IS IN ME REPEATING ITSELF

in

tendrils

of

spirit,

making it a riffle of soul

and

S O A P
O
P
E
R
A

of serious dark passionate brows
and hormones and meat.

WHAT

IS

WRONG

WITH

HAPPINESS?

the flatworm asks

and the owl hoots while the eagle
tears up the rabbit.

TAKE

A

DEEP

BREATH,

let it be a big picture

made in all imaginable senses.
Feel of the last quiver in the muscles
and jerk of the sinews in the leg
under the long scaled
fingers.   Talons clutched
into the furry neck.   Whistle
of expelled air.   Sight of big
brown eyes.   Smell of rabbit
blood.   Pink inside
of the beaks of downy chicks.
A
raven's
quark and
visual flash of baboon below
on
a
log
and spaces
of nothingness in protein
molecules.
Acacia thorns.   The biochemical
synergy of hunger
filling itself in smooth ebull-
ience marching to the music
of stars seen from night-roosting
over the edge of the cliffs.
Without sense it looks
like disorderly flames,
chaos,
complexity,
demon warriors, toad men, combustions
of petroleum in small chambers.

WITH

THE

SENSORIUM

broken

into
particles

it is
everything

looking up through dark brows at
itself
while a babe coos in a bedroom
and a lover is born

during

the earthquake.

One wing beats
with a smooth angry joyful
sound and the beak closes on
neck fur.   Perfume
of rabbit in the midst
of the overwhelming purring
that is the backdrop, the basic
sound of the unhearable mantra
carved out of lotuses and hummingbirds'
heartbeats
and the early
universes
at the beginning
of the lightning flash.
Raindrops hanging on plum leaf buds.
Sunlight and moon light on the craggy
redwood bark

and the smell of the car,
inside of the car,
dusty felt and ersatz velvet,
as it drives through the cliffs
of the desert.   Skull on the tabletop.
Squares of woven straw rugs.
Point Lobos as it always is
with a whale skeleton
and molecules
of Robinson Jeffers'
breath and shoe soles
looking
up
out
of my eyes
(sensing back and outwards into
a vision)
at the camera.
Beautiful toes in the shower.

WHAT

INTENSITY

OF

CONSCIOUSNESS

in everything;

NO,

IT
IS
everything.

Wet streams over the feet
on the metal floor
with smell of Roquefort
from another coterminal dream
of the original dimensions
beaming PASSION into
meat,
muscular meat.
Reaching out into stars
and down into stars
inside of stars.
No collar on the worn shirt.
Poems about high heels and a baby
on velvet

in a flash of sun.
Grinning out from his little cap
and sweater.
Monkey in the barn with the horses
of instruction while the black
'34 Ford boils over in the snow
and big green-brown tadpoles
waft through the pool
over their shadows.
A dot of light in each shadow
proves it.
Taste of Butterfinger bars in
the bright hot sun, like
silver, and patterns of lichens
over the volcanic rock hills
in red yellow green blue brown
black. A LAUGH
OF
PASSION
with the nothingness of meat
expanding in all directions

as the extension of them.
Big blue-black jay imitating the hawk's
                call.
                It's

                    a

                bluff

                    a

                cliff

                    a

                ledge

        beating like a heart

        from outside where it emulates
        itself, limited only by senses.
        Let there be ten trillion of them
            and like light everything
                    is everything
                in an illusion of infinite flatness
        in all directions and writhing
                    most
                    lucidly
                in meat
            and doorknobs
        of brass and face-shaped galaxies.
            So quaint
            so old-fashioned
as sweet and sour as Grandma's sex life
with clear wings of liberty and joy.
    Just the air in the room outside the ears

            is

            EVERYTHING

and he knows it in this lion state
that
it's the grumbling purr,
smooth as invisible quicksilver,
as the sulphur stone falls
in
to
it
eternally
endlessly,
forty trillion years.
A tiny sore bump on the tip
of the tongue.   The endless Hamlets,
and Duchesses of Malfi and Laurels
and Hardys and Abbotts and
Costellos.   Pirate ships and winged
daggers, smell of sardines
and baked beans or lima bean soup
with hamhocks
growing
like assemblages
from the blackness of the mystery.
No
color
at
all
not even
black
or a purr.
Nowhere manifest and vibrant
dull and glossy,
smelling like an old rock
that has been battered half smooth
by the stream
with deep eyes staring from the dramas
of meat behind the eyes.

It goes on and on endlessly
         but there is no it
             except the presence
      and no presence but passion
or courage.   And no passion
      or courage.   Even laughter!
Laughter shaped like a purr experiencing
      the wings and talons
             of itself
still mortal in the death screech
             of the rabbit.
      The lion is invisible but
             hardly less there
and History marches with banners
      and Wagnerian songs through
the small spaces between fingers
      lying upon chunky fingers
         on the smooth wooden tabletop.
      Smell of meat and coffee
      and black Spanish cigarettes.
The lower lip knows everything.
      Especially fear.   Sculpture
      of fear making cliffs of passion
         and courage.   Smell of pot
in the car.   Paintings of sailing ships
      over mantels on painted blue
and white waves.   Maya and molecules
      and nothing are the same and

         here I am

             in
         quarks
             and
         quasars
      always unseen

in everything:
spirit
descended
in
to
matter
in
a
glitter
of
courageous
fear
and pride looking
for real souls
to eat
as
I
sail.
BANG
goes
the
BLUE-BLACK GUN,
"Fuck you, right in your face,"
pours
up
from
the
D
E
E
P
NESS
spreading out before
consciousness

D
E
E
P
N
E
S
S

flowing out of and into baby meat
as the pussywillows open in a thicket
of skinny tendrils and delicate gray
soft fur with the rippling sound
of the stream running over rocks
fallen from the cliffs while
the hawk whistles above
the madrone tree and flaps
her wings three times, both at once,
to catch up with her mate.
It happened here on a carpet
of
MOSS.
Swifts fly high, whistling and mating
in air in the smoky
summer sunset.
Below the cliff
littered with carved stones
and remains
of
walls
is the plaza.   Cats walk
over the grass, moving
from tree to tree.
A peacock
called here.
It is all a garden, a dance
growing out of myself.

                    ALL
                    WILD
                    and
                    ALL
                  PERFECT
            with no need to be.
    BUT PASSION AND COURAGE
                  AND FEAR
                    all
                   speak
             of something else.
        There is no enigma because
            it all is confrontation.
    Hound dogs and sound of heaters running.
          Rabbit blood.   The camera.
      The high red-brown cliffs of the desert
             carved into sculptures
        of ancient kings and queens sitting
               on chairs of matter,
                  backs erect,
          and eyes looking out of the child
          way back in the smell of incense
            and tadpole ponds and dirty
          butts.   These are the fingers
            lying on the other stubby
             fingers.   Each one of them holds
          more consciousness than a lower
            lip or a brain.   While everything
      whites itself out into what
                is there.   It's just
          entropy with hunger pressing
               against it.   Shaping
            it into what it is, was, will be,
        melting into its tathagatian
                   self.

ONE

drop of blood
on the talon and a spray
of bloody fur on the breast.
Flat as stars cut out of tinfoil,
curly as memory growing
out of its interwinding with experience
while I imagine the lion roar
on Christmas Eve.   Not far away
are crocodiles in the river,
and the sly fast ones under
the bed,
and little turtles with round, flat
tin bodies stare from
these eyes in a dream
at a board game with stick pegs
carved out of cedar from
Solomon's groves.
Blackberries growing over graves.
Old men living in the forests
with pheasants and odd
cries of ruby-crowned kinglets
and thin catfish transparent as glass.
All there in the iris

WHICH
IS
THE
WHORLING,

WHORLING
CONDENSATION

of
the

moment
into the purr and feather of hands
with the mouth slightly open
in a pose.
Real as fear and courage,
as
prudent
as a grasshopper
or whirlwind.   Smell
of Blake's molecules all over
Job in the Old Testament.
Jakob Böhme as drunk as Jesus!
Swedenborg telling Sir Hans Sloane
that birds in dreams are souls.
Look
at
each
one
carefully,

vet
it.

Experience!
Moving through consciousness
is
as
dull
as Technicolor feathers
flowing over mirrors
reflecting every passion and desire
and
frustrated
HUNGER

looking up through the brows

WHILE
THE BELL CHIMES.

Dark clouds pour
    over the hill.
The city is the whirr of the air
        in shapes of cars and trucks
and riverbeds stood on end
        with windows and breasts
        and hats in elevators
        over the greensward.   Hiss goes
the city while the redwood grove
        is calm, turned into itself,
    in a hiss or a purr.   Dark brows
and vacant stars containing everything
    like the thicket of pussywillows
    in gray fur and the white
    blossoms of the plum tree
            bursting nearby.
            IT'S
            ALL
            STARS
        turning into a flow
of laughing dragons
with red scales and chests
        pouring over the edge
        of the brain
        coming
            up
            from
        the soles of the feet.
Knot after knot at the base
        of the cortex
            creating
                an
            attention

stage
focused on itself.
Sporophytes in the dark, bright
green moss
smirk
at the oak trees.
Mothers show sharks
to children.
L
A
M
B
S
stand next to fences
in Iceland and planes
land in the cold foggy
darkness
of
WHERE.
Where the growling is heard
while the feathers beat
and move with the ruffle
of the intake of air.
Toadmen sit on the fallen tree
by the baboon.   A baby
cries out with need
for love and milk.   The earth's
crust shakes and the walls
slip.   It all happens
by the young man's ears.   Dramas
in the sky of the room.
Plots of river gods and goddesses
and princes and queens.
Blue-black bullet in the head
of a President.
Self coming out like the CLOUD.

Cloud of faces.
Personality is grimaces
and holdings of muscles.
Gratuitous, well-trained
and in pain.
The Amtrak is a person
as
much
as
people
ARE.
Let it be the flesh
that is self.
HOLD,
let this
moment
never
cease.
But it never was,
eternally.
Raindrops on gray planks
and smell of old cashmere
sweaters where the rat gnaws
the luggage case.
The fingers slip up the other sleeve.
The camera clicks.
Photographer grins.
Soul is the elimination
of personality.
Soul invents soul
like the deep cloud
of somewhere else.

DRIVING

THE

CAR

IS

PERSONALITY.

enshrined.

The poem shows
nothing absent.
The knuckles and the pen
are a shadow
on a page
in the swirl
and the scroll spins.
Hunger and courage are ends
of the same worm
that the robin pries
from the golf course.
Night is weighed in the scale
in the room as
the white plum petals
F
A
L
L
into designs of rats
drunk in the branches.
The crossing of plane roars
lead to the old windowsill
and the purr it makes
in the eagle's beak.
This is it and it's all perfect,
imperfect,
never was,
nowhere
but a glossy brown Jeep
station wagon.

The cliff edge above
 the glittery silver flash
  ocean of something
    else.
   MOVE
    ON

   WITH
    BIG
   LOOPS

 of blue-black scaled biceps
  in a rosy aura of shimmer,
   or crunch of woven straw
  under the boot heel.
Walking through reflections of empty streets.
  There's no conflict in memory.   It's all here
   where it never was.   Laocoön loops
of streetlights and motes of dust in eyes
    long gone into the future.   A bearded
man listens, imagining childhoods in Mexico
      while the room purrs there in the middle
of the wing beats and makes a lengthening
      growl.   In front of the bookcase.
Smell of mackerel baking.   Leg of mutton.
   Diapers. The child's big face in the doorway.
     Babes singing in hallways.   Big land turtles
pulling ornate red chariots over shining wood
     F
     L
     O
     O
     R
     S
  on the riverbank.
 Mud of all kinds making veils.

The parasite of personality drops away
as the muscles, and the muscles
of spirit, loop and throw out coils,
exfoliate tendrils.   Comprehension.
Understanding the taste of red purple
grapes with green flesh
and the seed nestled in there where
the tongue glides in something
written while high
in the old days.
Shaped like a star in all directions,
the
moment
blasts
and dodders
and skims
through everything.
Outside of everything
containing it.   The dentist
drills on the mountain range
as if it were mute and dumb.   Dumb
and mute, not hearing him.   The nurse
giggles in flattery at the base
of the cliff where the snaggle-
toothed Indians push the Jeep
through mudbank.   Lightning
crash.   Pearls in the lotus bud.
M
A
N
D
A
L
A
S

of containers stacked
for pickup with the milk
tanks. A wall of cicadas
singing turned into a roar
of the ears. Fears of nothing
and whirr of wooden yo-yo.
As the hand slides from the other
hand up the sleeve. The smile
is vacant and sly and knowing
and deep. Soulful. Freed of personality.
Freed of tendrils being the tendrils.
Solid personality
of gold and ivory and donkey fur
laughing at itself
like
courage
being cheap.
In
the
air
Bushmen's dreams
of gazelles turning to eagles
in the roar and the purr and the roar.

ROAR.

Roar

behind
the
eyes
beyond
parturition
on the other side
of

                    the
                   lost
               dimension

            in this one

                    B
                    E
                    F
                    O
                    R
                    E

                  meat

              conceived

                   of
                   its

                hungers.
         At the foot of the cliff
      beside his ears in the room
        the cloud bursts, straight
        and flowing shapes of blue-purple
        from the old skull top
            as the goddess
            upward flows
         from the perineum
      to all the dimensions bound
                   in

                    O
                    N
                    E

imaginary ball.
Where there is no imagination
but the madman calling
through the corridors
of his lost teeth.
The young man's sly smile
of passion and courage
and hopeful fear.
Snail trails on the sidewalk
in the silver wind.
Screams from a lost love
on cold empty streets
and loving kisses in
midnight playgrounds.
The chunky fingers slide
up the sleeve
as the room fills with feathers
and blood and purring
roars.
The central nervous system is shaped
like the Milky Way.
And the odor almost like
licorice.

AFTERWORD TO "PORTRAIT OF THE MOMENT"

I have finished "Portrait of the Moment," and each day's lines seemed like a miracle, a miracle of writing and of consciousness, and each day that I reread it, preparatory to writing the new lines, I tapped my foot to the music I heard in it.

I wrote sitting on this couch, with the sun through the windows on my shoulders or the sound of rain in my ears as the plum blossoms budded and then opened day by day in January, February, and March. It was written after walking through the trees and forests and streets of houses and with the calls of jays and juncos and redtail hawks, and with airplanes passing over. It was all written spontaneously and without changes, and not for the sake of writing from the unconscious (as in the first section, "Stanzas in Memory") but to pursue a single moment and to put it into being as a poem. I wrote to explore a single moment that was in my mind, and immediately it became progressively clearer that *the moment* is every moment and is all moments in all times and places. I could be in *all those moments* in the moment in my mind and imagination and hand and pen. The moments before the invention of time were as close to me as the moments of the present and the moment of the new future. I was meat. I was memory. I was inspired by an exploration that came to me and explored me. I had intimations of the dimensions that have disappeared and I realized again that Artaud is one of the greatest poets because of his use of his mind/body and his psychosis as both his person and his tool to understand the universe. It is understandable to all of us when we use our passions and our energies as acts. Compared to Blake this is a modest poem and it has filled me with the riches of sense and space that are always there. Perhaps it will please someone else and they may appropriate it for their own consciousness.

I once found a dolphin skull on a beach in Baja Mexico; I kept the skull and sometimes looked through it, through the eyes, through the foramen magnum, and through the blowhole on the dorsal surface. I thought of Goethe looking at Schiller's skull or Hamlet looking at Yorick's. Perhaps this can be such an instrument—but it is more of a remembrance of life than a memento mori.

RARE
ANGEL *(1975)*

for William Jahrmarkt

FOREWORD

Rare Angel tracks vertically on the page and is Oriental in the way that a Japanese poem may be written running down a scroll. The selves that comprise our whole being may play over the poem, as if it were a tape, and make prints and new codings. One's selves can reach out and speak as the pages move past them. The poem gives birth to itself from the substrate of the physique by writing out muscular and body sensations which are the source of thought.

Rare Angel is about the interwoven topologies of reality. It reaches for luck—swinging out in every direction. It is about the explosion going on.

Walking the city streets the old buildings sink into nonexistence and the new buildings rise up. The flow of change is palpable and exciting. It is thrilling to be in this waste and destruction and re-creation. That is one of the sensualities of American culture. Our primate emotions sing to us in the midst of it. No one grants credit for the brilliance we burst in.

Whitehead says, "But when mentality is working at a high level, it brings novelty into the appetitions of mental experience. In this function, there is a sheer element of anarchy. . . . It introduces a higher appetition which discriminates among its own anarchic productions. Reason appears."

And *Rare Angel* appears like an organism with dark eyes and bristly spotted fur and shining teeth. It is comprised, as our cells are, of memories of Pleistocene mammoth hunts and of molecules from toy plastic umbrellas.

Bio-alchemical investigations—concerns with the shapes and meanings of bodies—are inseparable from poetics. Experience in all times and places is the mainstream. The ability to sensorially perceive without the constraint of traditional proportions is the joy of the yogin, the adept, the poet, and the scientist of meat.

AND SO WE STRETCH OUT

(it is a muscular sensation
from the neck and shoulders
through the arm . . .

AND SO WE STRETCH OUT
and raise ourselves above our own
black factories.
And we are not in search of poetry but luck
that is ten trillion Milky Ways
that make a molecule within our chest
or a billion feathered songs sung
from horseback on a bison hunt
WHERE BEAMS OF LIGHT
flash here and there
and make new colors out of dust
that we emit in Fields of Thought.

THEN I KNOW THAT I AM NATURE
where'er I walk
or drink or think.
I AM THIS SWART PEARL
of Space
TURNED
INSIDE
OUT!

———————————

ALL STRANGE STRIPED
CREATURES SLITHERING
through the roots
grin and dance
TO
NEW MUSIC.
I am THEY or THEM!

AND
NOW
I am the man within this movie hall
where samurai are slashing with their swords
and flashlights play upon the concrete walls
and toilets smell like modern kitchens.

AND
I can NEVER let myself
go wild, for I remember
I AM ALL.
BUT NOW I AM CLEARER THAN THE CLOUD I EVER WAS.
NOW I AM HERE AND SMILINGLY BELIEVE
EACH THING.

SURELY YOU KNOW THIS IS ME. I CAN BE
told by my naked cock standing up
as I leap through space and fall
on everything I am. LIKE YOU,
WE
are all
and *everything*.

WOLF VIOLETS HOWL!

DREAMS OF OCTOBERS STRANDED ON
BLACK SHALE BEACHES.

Blackberries lying in snow.
Giant snapping turtles in hot, muddy water.
Fingers crossing the moon.
Scent of jasmine.
Tongue on flesh of cling peaches.

GRANDMOTHERS AND GRANDFATHERS FUCKING.
It is all as lovely

AS

A

PIECE
of fluff
THAT FLOATS.

.

.

.

.

.

.

.

.
.
.
.
.
.
.
.

THIS IS THE STUFF! WE ALWAYS KNOW IT IS.

THIS IS THE EXPLOSION
happening all
around us . . .

WE CREATURES
AT OUR CAVE LIPS . . .
(selves are caverns)
hang
down, draped
from ourselves
like waves,
or
stand up
like scarlet mushrooms
in the glowworm's light,

or swim
in cold
rivers underground
through the limestone
made of dots
formed in star clusters . . .

HELLO. HERE IS MY HAND I REACH TO YOU.
(It is something like a paw.)

THIS HUGE PIECE FLASHING BY
IS A CITY MIMING LIFE!

The sword slashes
through nineteen
bodies

             —it is one
                dream
               of what
              we want.

                 YOU

                KNOW

                  ME

              BECAUSE

                 I'M
             WATCHING

                 YOU.

You have toes and breasts.

YOU COULD SAY I
wish to be
gentle, sweet, and lovable,
and that would be true, but it
would
stifle
all that matters

if it
became
a code
to live by

WHILE
all this

happens!

Faces peeping from rocks.
Clusters of nothing forming particles.
Rainbows over daisies.
Men watching eagles.
Coils of being turning
to new scents.

MESSAGES IN SEARCH OF SUBSTRATE.

Black zebras swallowing rubies,

Night hawks by barns.

AND THEN PICTURE THE FIELDS THAT STREAM
FROM THAT,
and the clouds they make—or squirms of energy

and relationship. I know
that it *cannot* be
distorted.
It all (as it explodes
or creates
itself—
or
anything)
is surely the messiah. I
fly by
without moving
in it.

Steady,

steady.

STEADY AS SHE GOES!

AND THEN I AM SITTING IN THIS WHITE TRUCK
AT THE CURB OF NOWHERE
where the rug is blood
AND
I
watch for you
because you'll know me.
And that is anthropoid or hominid
to always watch for ourselves
in the other's eye. To always
seek a mirror in hope that it will
FLATTER.
We
SCATTER
in the endless search

for trophies of the instant
because
they taste so sweet

but
it is
better
yet

to crack the scroll of time
instead!

— — — — — — — — — —

AND REACH INTO IT AS WE STRETCH!

WE

ARE
REAL

DRAGONS
OF OUR LUCK.

We swirl out what we are and watch for its return.

AND THE PHARISEES BRAND US WITH
TORTURED WORDS
in hope that they'll cause us anguish
for the grief we've hurled
(unknowingly

or

not)
at them. They drift
around like twisted demons.
MESSAGES OF SEXUAL JOY
we never asked for
(and

are

lies)
slither up and down the walls
in formless colors outlined
only
by the shapes of our desires.

WHILE THE WAR DRAGS ON
and little tufts of smoke
in passing eyes
remind us of the sizeless nearby battlefield.

•

Mutate into albinos.
Everything is cut
away
that was useless.
What's left
is
turned
to
new
nerves.

WE KNOW *THAT* IS HAPPENING TO US

((OR THE OPPOSITE))!

EVERY EXPOSURE

to

new condition

is our interwinding
with the welcoming messiah.
EACH
MOUNTAIN
is
a
breast
we fall upon.

IT IS NOT ENOUGH TO SAY THAT EVERYTHING IS US.
YOU ARE AS CLOSE AS MY TOUCH.
FUR.
MUSK.
MAROON PLUSH IN DARKNESS.
Scent of popcorn.
Rivulet of blood.
White buildings in the shroud of fog.
Amphipods in the icy tide.
Fronts of buildings with their back ends torn away.
Black man who sells me cola in his cave.
Angered
child.
Everything
winds in and out
in imitation
of our gut—
or vice versa!
It's more than we can know, except
by rubbing on it.
THERE
ARE
CONCEPTS
just beyond
our grasp
and we're always
at their edge,
when we care to be.
(And I cannot help but care
to be,
for that's my pleasure
and my claim
to what I see.)

TOUCH OF COLD WIND IN BRIGHT SUNLIGHT.

Smell of oil.

Dead fish on cracked ice

and

light *almost* trapped within the sun.

MEMORIES FROM ICELAND MIXED WITH IMAGININGS OF INDONESIA.

GUN
KNIFE
LIFE
STUN
BUN
STRIFE
WIFE
FUN
STAR
TOMB
BOOK
FAR
WOMB
LOOK,
everything is flowing,
everything can see . . . All waves
have eyes!
Literature and life can melt together!

Crows float in air over Douglas fir trees.

Thrones of carved jade in mountain caverns.
Smell of ponds in springtime.
(Darting of the pollywog.)
Daddy-longlegs caressing in the moonlight.
Pressure of moonbeams on surf.
Red macaws sacrificed in clouds of copal incense.

Fractured surfaces of flint made into an edge.
Towers spouting oil.

Speeding tortoises of metal.
Eyes and nose holes moving on flat walls.

Miracles present themselves
for our benefit and we make
of them what we will.
WE
NEED
TO KNOW
that all these separations
make one thing,

or to learn about the illusion that we call *one*.
Or to see, like Kilroy, over the edge of something.

RAVEN'S FEATHER. EAGLE'S CLAW. EVERY
SONG EVER CHANTED
by the whale hunter
is a collector's item
and wafts like mountain fog
from node to node before becoming clouds.
EVERY
BACKWARD
LOOK
puts us in touch with sentiment,
and hurts less than peering forward,
for tomorrow is the shadow of today.
Even the blue jay
gloats over his stash
of brass buttons. See the octopus play
with the exoskeleton
of his prey.

The statement's convolution
confounds what is already done.

Bulldozed hillsides.

Scarlet flower bugles on the mountain top
overlook the graveyard.

Such elegant music when we make it
(for poets call it music)
surprises
US
in the act
of what we do.

The hand plays hide and seek
with the eye, and we grow
great brains
in honor of the game.
Then we dance and the music
follows at our footsteps
and we stop to listen
as it passes by.
WE
HEAR
THE MUSIC
OF
our selves!

Call it animal nature—or name it Civilization.

Sᴘᴀʀʀᴏᴡ ʜᴀᴡᴋ ꜱᴋᴜʟʟᴄᴀᴘ. ʟɪɢʜᴛɴɪɴɢ ʙᴏʟᴛ
THAT PASSES
THROUGH THE HAND.
WAVES OF CREATURES FLOATING
AT THE EDGE OF FIRE
dive into the air and bound
through space with grace
we nearly comprehend.

Bodies: brown and black and white all blended.
Hoofed and leaping.

TURQUOISE.

CHROME!

Berries and Packards all exploding, lined
with fur of force fields.

DESTRUCTION UNROLLED UPON THE PLEISTOCENE
where we stride in luscious comfort,
and love our children,
hug our pets,
experience
the
alchemy of being.

THE FEW OF US LIKE WAR CHIEFS
AND LOVE-GOD PRINCES
STAND ON THE PRECIPICE WITH FOLDED ARMS.
THIS
LIFE
has
been

nothing

for
me
but
pleasure.

The worst adversity
is only a length
I measure.
I direct creation of my bed of eider blackness
and drink the juice of apples
as I sup on flesh of crabs.
I
hold great minds
that lived before me
in my hands.
I KNOW THE MEANING OF THE POWER
THAT IS CHANNELED FOR ME. AND I
calmly watch the poisons
splashed across the land.

I HAVE CUT THROUGH THE HUMANE SURFACE
and I know all men and women
(and they
know me
for I
am them).
WE POUR FORTH OUR WANTS
in the center of this tornado.
Nothing can tear down
what we are
—we only color it with intellective lies.

I
WAS
RIGHT:
WE
ARE
LOVES AND HUNGERS!!!
—Delicate at moments, murderous and murmurous at others. Our
CRIES

are songs and howls
that we make into the sizzling air.

FOR KNOWLEDGE OF WHAT IS TRULY HAPPENING
(beyond our sense of fingertouch or ear)
we must read the walls
while they stand there
amidst the great unrolling,
and study the positioning
of garnets
on the boulder.

THE RETOPOLOGIZING IS RIGHT NOW! WE ARE WAVES
and Princes
in
the
surge!

LIKE ALL MEN AT ALL TIMES, WE ARE ELF
AND FAIRY FOLK!

HEAVY FOOTED AND LUMPISH OR LIGHT AND
DANCING ON THE FLOCCULENCE OF CLOUDS.
WITH DIM WITS OR EYES BRIGHT AND PIERCING,
the hungers are always all the same.
There is little change
except in the counting of the power
that flows to the lip of our ledge. The same
sacrifices evoke the new gods once again.
Zigzag knife or tracer bullet. Kisses made

between the sheets of a perfumed bed.
Little loving creatures there upon our laps
with big brown eyes.

NEW DRUGS
always in demand

to bring the loving god to hug us
as we dive to him and breathe in the embrace.
BUT
we are the Gods!
And not because we say so
in faustian paranoia. Or because
there is a wish to be.
The gift grew, and Luck
can push it further.

THE URGE TO DO IT FEEDS THE LUST TO GROW
BY MEANS OF SWIRLING
into spaces.
Silver towers in cold sea mist.
Severed arms.
Pink elephants and cherubim holding purple plastic flowers.

THOUGHT
is
a
muscular
sensation
pouring outward like
pseudopods with feathered hoofs.
Each hoof taps at the tacks
that press the scroll of the instant
flat upon the field of nothingness.

OH, HOW BEAUTIFUL!

BEAUTIFUL!

The wolf howl on the frosty night.

The rat upon the branch who eats
the cherry blossoms.

Grinning otter sleeping on the waves.

WE
cannot
be
sure
which constellations
open wide the fields like velvet drapes.
I only

watch. Driving
in it. Parking by
the gray curb
that is a universe
for the sensoriums
of
nematodes.
((Or parking by
the gray curb
that is a universe.))
Or
putting a black boot
in the rippling water
of a childhood day.
Or
hearing rain on an umbrella
in soundless space.

THEN I KNOW I AM NATURE, AS TOPOLOGY
UNROLLS ABOUT ME.
Forests turning
into books and rugs.
Things
are carbonized.
Cinders remain where life was/
but power remains
in the frame
of new shapes.
Till I,
TOLTEC-I,
AM CHANGED

and barely recognize
my
chubby past
and well-loved toys.
For now I fool with alchemy
to blast my being
past the explosion's burping edge.
EVERYTHING IS NOW A *REAL* TOY.
HAWK CRY AND TRUCK ROAR
are an open door
to just one
purpose:

TO
FOLLOW
DOWN
WHAT
MY
BODY
KNOWS
and pour out like shoulders

from a neck,

OR
LIE LIKE
A PAIR OF DICE
ON WHITE VELVET,

OR DREAM LIKE BLOSSOMS ON AN APPLE BOUGH,

OR KISS GOOD MORNING TO THE MORNING,

or flow like dew around the nests of sleeping mice!

RACING THROUGH THE TUNNELS UNDER SNOW.

Hailstones the size of apricots.

Children singing in the sundown.

L OVELINESS
OF GOLD FLAKES
SCATTERED INTO ERMINE.
.

OR
AM I A DEMON
with my head thrown
back and mouthing
words from this cave
of faces? or am I
AN ANGEL
(all sweet and bright)
(warm, solid, real)
with arms crossed
and hands on biceps?

The poem that I'm writing is like a museum of living nudibranches
(a long line of clown messiahs) describing TOLTEC-ME and baby-me
—and the way the surface of the Earth is an energy explosion that
removes the Pleistocene and leaves only cinders in the shapes of book-
ends, rugs, and tractors. And even that (sadly) is a part of my "spiritual"
development. So the poem has to rise by making a swooping swing so
that the whole is finally (perhaps) a sublime perception locked into itself
and reaching out. It is numberless trials that make a conscious and
unconscious feedback loop.

A
PALACE FOR LARGE BLACK ANTS
at the base of the walnut tree.

Flick of swords slashing brows.

Flashlight beams playing over concrete.

My imagination

(only)
reaches warmth
across
the space.
Who knows what she sees.
The huge hairy animals haul themselves
along the plain and stop and eat
the bushes. By the water hole
men leap up out of silence
swinging clubs and screaming.
The hairy creatures stand in wonder
and terror and faintest
flicker of admiration for the painted faces . . .

So NOW IT'S SERIOUS,

YOU SAY.

You say it is serious.

You say it pours into itself
like honey poured from cup to cup.

THINGS ARE WHAT THEY ARE:
WAVES OF STARS OR DOTS.

I
KNOW
ALL
THAT!

The net of constellations
is as serious
(or laughable)
as I am.

THE

SILHOUETTE

OF

A

PELICAN

DIVING

BEAK

FIRST

into

WAVES.

Red and gray and blue
reflections flickered back and forth.

Dead friends speaking to me.

Sailing ship mirrored in its own wake.

SAND DOLLARS.

GIANT CACTI.

Huge rivers bursting through the mountains.

WAVES THAT TAKE THE SHAPE OF WATER
cradling the surge of salmon schools . . .

Ripples that take the form of typewriters
or of men . . .

SIGNS THAT SAY:

HOTEL

HOTEL

HOTEL

or almost sentimentally:

Coca-Cola.

Over-replicated children sneer and make love-signs
at one another.
The old high way of thinking in clarity
is drowned by lack of judgment
and now we formulate in clouds
of color, heaps of scents,
and all the textures
planned
by
creative genius.

AHHHHHHHH-H-H-H-H-H-H-H-H-H-H—
we know we're love gods
in pain.

EMPTY HAND REACHING THROUGH SPACE.

THE UPSURGE OF SELF-AFFIRMATION.
Smiles returned by beautiful faces.
Sunbeam gleaming in a dusty room.
Skulls lined side by side upon a table:
man, dolphin, raccoon.
Flying lemurs eating coconut flowers in moonlight.

JET FIGHTERS IN MID-AIR FIRING ROCKETS
AT EACH OTHER.

Flaming horses in the surf.

ANOTHER SPOT—SOMEWHERE
ELSE IN ANOTHER
SWIRL OF SPACE
or
untouchable
dimension
and I am writ upon it in modes of senses
that I do not comprehend.
It's here beneath my foot
or lost behind
another Milky Way.
The fire burns caverns in a cardboard box.
Black edges curl inward in red flames . . .

The sound of surf makes grottos
in my mind. Sand beneath
my elbow. Boulders of silicon
and serpentine and smooth crushed shell.
The helicopter is a bar of ruthless sound
across it all. The fall

TAKES
THE PRISONER
looping thirty thousand feet
with hands bound behind his back
while crowds of feasting gods
are singing his goodbye.
The jay turns over a brass button.

THE MONSTER OPENS HIS BLUNT FACE—EYES WIDE!
Snags of fur blow around his snout
in the savanna wind. Dragonflies
dart away from the water hole. The coppery
horsehair snakes move blindly—and indifferent—
frightening mosquito larvae with the clouds
of sediment. Water striders move back

among the cattails. The beast screams wheezingly
with fear and alarm. He raises one clawed
arm—half-turns—shit pours
from him into the pond.
One man rips him open
with the flint.
Blood pours like a little waterfall
from a fur mountain.

THEY YELL WITH GLEE
distorting stripes
of ochre and green
upon their faces.

The baby raven listens from his nest
on a nearby cliff.
Vultures think about it overhead.

Two things grow together in the darkness.

ᴀɴᴅ ʏᴇᴛ ɪᴛ ɪs ɢʀᴇᴀᴛ ʟᴏᴠᴇ
—ʀᴇᴀʟ ᴘʜʏsɪᴄᴀʟ ᴀᴛᴛʀᴀᴄᴛɪᴏɴ—ᴛʜᴀᴛ ᴍᴀᴋᴇs
us what we are.
Each cell is an inheritor
of earlier loves.
ɴᴏᴛ
ᴏɴᴇ
ʟᴏᴠᴇ
but many formed each cell
of every
being!
Each cashmere gesture reflects it.

Every time I reach or withdraw in kindness.

ᴇᴠᴇʀʏ ᴘᴜssʏᴡɪʟʟᴏᴡ ɪɴ ᴛʜᴇ ᴍᴀʀsʜ
ᴏʀ ᴍᴀᴅ ᴠɪᴏʟᴇᴛ ɪɴ ᴛʜᴇ ᴍᴇᴀᴅᴏᴡ.

ᴇᴠᴇʀʏ ɢɪʀᴀꜰꜰᴇ ᴀɴᴅ ᴀᴜᴋ ᴀɴᴅ ᴊᴀɢᴜᴀʀ . . .

Every bat and great blue whale
and planetoid
or red giant.

ᴇᴠᴇʀʏ sᴇᴛ ᴏꜰ ɢᴇsᴛᴜʀᴇs ᴍᴀʀᴋᴇᴅ ꜰʀᴏᴍ ᴏɴᴇ ᴘᴏɪɴᴛ
ᴀɴᴅ sᴛᴏᴘᴘᴇᴅ ᴀᴛ ᴀɴᴏᴛʜᴇʀ
becomes a cloud
that is a field
in all directions that we know
and many others. And we
write upon it in calligraphy
of what we are. But only
guess how
to reread it.
Then that makes a field within
and all around the other.

THE
SWORD
IS MADE FOR BEAUTY;
DUTY
KILLS.

BUT death is only at one point upon a field.

THE CLOUD IS A MOHAIR SHAPE
of interwoven
constellations
that
comprise
each other.

LOVE AND HUNGER COMPRISE HATRED.
HATRED AND LOVE
join to be hunger. Hatred and hunger are love.
It is a verbal exercise to show
that we
are made
in subtler ways
than our Platonic statements.
Everything
all melted down
and glossy-glassy
becomes an ethic like a green
plastic Parthenon
and

it

WILL

NEVER BEAT

OLD AGE OR DEATH!

No vacuum cleaner or opinion brings escape
or Liberation.

NO GURU
OR
MOSES
BRINGS
you
any
news
but your own winged smile!

WE ARE AS FREE
as
everything
around
us!
Candles burning in the twilight.

Trucks growling in the dawn.

Floors rippling in an earthquake.

Embroidery upon the lips of clouds.

Thunderstorm above a cornfield.

Scent of pink silk and encyclopedias.

THE LEOPARD SEAL DIVES UPWARD IN THE WATER
—CRASHES THROUGH THE ICE
AND GRABS THE PENGUIN.

Hot penguin blood on cheeks and whiskers.

Veils of plankton.

Mysterious laughing faces buried in fire, earth, water, air.

"Know thy self."
But the brain is not
truth's organ
and we find
there is no tathagata
but the all
we are.
The cloud is silky sexuality
or solid rock
or
empty nothing
filled
with smiles and frowns.

FREEWAYS GLOW
with their machine-gun automatic load:
CAR (*swish*) CAR (*swish*) CAR (*swish*) . . .

Our feet grow flat and human
and our hands more soft and subtle.

Then we can bring
out
the hungry tree shrew
with
his

swinging saber
in the darkened room

and move the physiology
of ancient bodies
in patterned colored light.

That is science in the guise of art
or entertainment.

That is all I am.

My trembling
makes me real.

how fine a thing is longing—or a hunger!

AND SYMPATHY IS HATRED FOR THE FAILING SELF.
Sympathy draws one body inside
another (as does hunger)
and makes love—
and many into one.
Genius
grinds all things
into infinite pieces
and scatters
them
in all times and places

with
organic sense
of what it is all about

—and then forgets and has a dream
about
A SILVER EGG.

CIRCLES OF LIGHT MOVE ON THE CONCRETE WALL
in blackness.

The curb in bright sunlight.
Sound of rain on an umbrella.
Abalone shell reflecting dawn.
Shimmering sunlight in a perfect room.
Blissful fantasies adrift.
Honeybee screaming in the dusty
grade-school window.

Soft leather purse with pennies in it.

Scent of candy stores and clack of castanets.

Deer moving in the mottled shade.

Hunters singing.

.
.
.
.
.
.
.
.
.
.
.
.

A PENGUIN WALKING ON THE ICE.

AND SO WE STRETCH OUT
and the muscular sensation moves
from neck and shoulders
through the arm
AND
THE
Real Poetry
comes in moments like the dawn
or instances of thoughtlessness
made bright by rich and blank
sensoriums.
Then all things lay themselves out
rich and shimmering
in full pigment
dappled by the light.

. •

I MEAN THE BED HAS WINGS AND CARRIES ME.
I smile as casually
as an otter
in the golden sleepy sun.
The wolf-dog in the vacant lot devours a cat
and wags his tail.

WE
LOVE
TO
WALK
THROUGH

ROOMS
OF
WHAT
WE ARE
and know the flesh is shaking in the air.

WE ARE EACH A LOVE GOD
dissolved
into reality
and searching for the frozen furnace
of the dissolution.

EVERY
LITTLE
THING
HAS
VISAGES
AND WINGS
or doesn't.

IT MATTERS TO US WHAT WE ARE AT THIS
(AND EVERY)

FLASHING INSTANT!

THE RABBIT CARES!
AS DOES THE OCTOPUS AND QUARTZ CRYSTAL!
A
hairless, purple head
pokes in from everywhere
and we name it *friend*.
We glide at ninety times the speed of light
on helixes
of hurricanes that pour
into the maelstrom.

We stack old wooden chairs
and put cigarette butts in the lips of moose heads.

I know there is a distance there
between
the I
and you.
Rocketships flash back and forth
from our fingers
in the darkened room.
The landscape is made of the bodies of trees
cut into strips.
There are
fighting people.
The men worship flowers
knowing they are blooms
themselves
and they pluck one another to make bouquets.

IN THE RICH WET CREVICES WHERE EVERYTHING
is just one life
the symbiosis starts.
Everything
coils
over

and
crumples—as if in preparation
for explosion.
Hugs together.
Creates a complex anchor-net.
Hurls itself out—as if to catch
the wings of Time
could matter.

CAN
WE
BE THAT DUMB
AND BEAUTIFUL?

ARE WE ALL FABLED BLONDES OF BLACKNESS
WITH DIAMONDS IN OUR HAIR?

"Why do all the wise beings on earth eat my ass, mine,
Antonin Artaud's?"

"And what in hell are we doing here?
Why in hell are we living?
And why are we alive?"

TO
READ
THIS
POEM
!
To pursue our luck
in aggregate complexities
of perception.
¿To open the chest wide so the Indian band
may pour out whooping in pursuit
of bison?

TO CREATE NEW TERRITORIES IN THE
SHAPES OF HANDS.
(To intertwine, to let all being fly.)

To build the battlefields and No Man's Lands
of Love.

To spray the scent of strawberries into interstellar space?
To coat almonds with smooth sugar.
To hold wet water snails.

—SO THAT *SELF* MAY BE SELF'S MESSIAH
EVERYWHERE!

It
comes slanting
all at once like

electric rain. They say
it does!

. . . .

To make a kind of pine cone.

A simple thing of facets.

Less than a buttercup.

Barely alive

but

breathing.

All torn up in new directions everywhere.

"Mass was invented to make human sexuality pass through
certain paths." (A.A.)

DÜRER, RAPHAEL, AND SHANG DYNASTY
CRAFTSMAN OF BRONZE.
All are concerned with babes, madonnas,
tigers, owls.
They are
hypnotized by
(*in love with*)
gorgeous
shapes
of moiling intricacy
—and show them flat
or in faint relief.

They leave the eye to move around
in the material mind.

Let the neuron eye-light
flow around
the body of
a sun bear.
Let the eye-light
charge
in no known form
through
no
known blackness.
Let the blackness be indigo and melt in silver.
OUT
OF
IT
COMES THE SHADOW
OF MY FACE
OR YOURS.
It gains dimension
—then becomes a cliff with firs
—then a planetoid.

Now it is a psychic submarine and dives
streaming into
everywhere.
Then it becomes a hand to write with white music
in the shadows.
Cars carve the freeway up with sounds.

When we lose ourselves it is death, and Luck enters.
REBORN!

Brown hills flow gently towards
the mud flats.
Seals face the sunset.

Limpets under boards.

The antlered worms are artisans of hunger.

W<small>E ARE ADDICTED TO OUR PERSONALITIES.</small>
(I AM!)
What pleasure then to let it go, and slide
away from all the pain.
But
then
WE ARE NOTHING
is the cry—
and that is right.

LOKI GETS THE LAST LAUGH.

We are hollow snakes in nowhere.
If the tanner comes
and takes the skin
then what is left
is the frost giant's grin
reflected on a glacier.

BLACKNESS
splits into two ravens,
Thought and *Memory.*
They
fly
forward
and settle on our shoulders.

The well stares up at us with one eye
and a trillion-billion facets
stir when the hazelnut
of personality drops in.

AND
THEN
THE SALMON LEAPS
AND EATS THE MAYFLY!

Sounds of motorcycles grinding on the peaks.
Feel of Autumn in the air.
Russet ripples.
Maid Quiet walking on the leafy forest floor.

THE CAVE WHERE CHILDREN PLAY
BENEATH THE GIANT STUMP.

And
—like art nouveau—
the black wings
make weird silhouettes
that we see between.
They tell me everything has a name
because the universes rub together.

An apple brushing on a feather.

THE LIKELIHOOD OF PERSONALITY IS IMPOSSIBLE.
BUT PROBABLE!
What other thing
would I have be *me*?
An abstract song sung by asteroids?
A rainy glaze upon a tropic forest
is
what
I am.
And I'm glad.

. . . .

THE NET THAT IS AN ANCHOR AND A SURGE
hurls itself out
as
if
the whole thing matters.
As it does, flames roll from the edges
in extreme slow motion.
It becomes more complex
than an aerial lichen
and the whole thing
catches fire.
WE
ARE
THE
FIRE
MEN!

We
are the eaters in the grassy lands
that enter forests for the sake of Deer.

We have tortured and eaten all warm-blooded
dragons
and sung our crazy songs
and found our corn, squash, wapato,
wheat and rice. We kissed goodbye to the antlered
giraffe and rhino. The last pink-haired
fairy armadillo
hides beneath a stone
in secret contact
with the final familiy of golden lion marmosets.

It
is sweet to be a Prince

with my heel upon this scene.

Boccherini, Mozart, Haydn, seven-stringed ch'in lute tinkle
on my sky-high porch.

Rare ANGEL (take a letter),

PINK RIPPLES ARE WAFTING FROM
THE LIGHTNING BOLT.
BLUE CLOUDS FLOAT AROUND IT ALL.
Horizons separate
with flesh drifting
in between.
Blue-purple waterfalls
drip down
upon the fields
that we
inhabit.

Drums beat in the middle distance.
Cock starlings squeak on rooftops.
Bearded students lounge
in damp cafes.

Envies and hungers beat upon the walls with leaden fists.
Substances become huge like visions
and then deplete themselves.
FIGURES
FLICK
INTO
THE
AIR
WITH FLASHING SWORDS!
Oriental profiles float
upon the walls.

And the whole conjoined
improbable unlikelihood
flips
up its edge
to catch

at Time
that passes.
The explosion
flows outward from
each direction.
The flames
are thawed
in giant
frigidaires.

DARKNESS
and
LIGHT
are
moved
from
place to place
in groaning boxes
filled with broken legs.

RARE ANGEL . . .

Black arts are smeared on April afternoons like toothy smiles

grinned at a fearful dog that cowers behind
a lattice porch.

BABY SMILES.
Taste of Drambuie.
Red cottages in mist.
Rowboats on a lake.
Giant logs afloat in surf.
The scent of kelp.
The lives
of sea anemones
on pilings.
The blank,
behemoth
metaphilosophies
of jellyfish
and sea cucumbers.

THERE!
Again I reach for you.
You, being warm and real, insist
that
I
know
what
YOU
think
is beautiful.
And I have no contradiction
but I'll always
search for some
other answer.
Whatever
it may be.

EVERYTHING
is what our senses
make it—
SORTING
THROUGH
THE SMOKE!

Being might slip out of its concealment
to become one thing
once again

OR
it may not.

BUT
you're swirling.

(WHIRLING
and settling like a flock of crows
around a party of blind chimpanzees
on a picnic.)
I can hear the sound but I cannot know
the patterns or the flights.
I can symbolize
but I cannot
speak of it.
I
do not
have the centers
—OR
THE SPIRIT-NEURONS—
to make the stream of words.
I get the message
but I do
not have the screens
to show the pictures.

I
HAVE
BEEN
EVERYWHERE
when it happened.

(It is beginning
to be over.)

The control room
is a stage prop.
Through the windows
we
can
see the sets.
They are real:

rubies, diamonds,
tulips, flames,
and fantasies,
and purple scarves,
and spider webs
and chocolate bars.

Only the simplest levers
fit our hands. I can
go up or down
and right and left
and fly and pour
and drip and flash
UNSTOPPABLE
AMONG THE CLOUDY STUFFS THAT MAKE
THIS SOLID THING.

We

know it.

ALL THE WORM TRAILS UNDERNEATH THE BARK
OF A GIANT FOREST
write a name in a script
I cannot translate.
And I do not care to.
Its existence
is a spirit's
secret name
AND
all lives lean
on each other.
They are clean and lean
and well known.
Like a chinchilla-bat with tentacles
they toss out strands
and at their tips
are a billion buffalos
or a fern forest
or the whisker of a ring-tailed cat
that is chewing on a mouse skull.
I
HAVE A MEMORY
OF A FRIEND LYING DEAD
IN A POOL OF BLOOD IN AFGHANISTAN.
A
pistol
in his hand.

He melts back in.

The mountain speaks to me
by being
as
a rose vine does.
Dead friends
are

clear
too.

The jay is gone.
He gloats over buttons.

A RAINBOW ROLLER COASTER.

An elephant's foot umbrella stand
is a sadder thing
than my friend's death.

The eyes of ducklings and their breath.

Gorillas sleeping in the forest.

Glaciers calving icebergs into the Arctic Sea.

ALL THINGS ARE MATTER WHEN MASS ARISES.
That which does not transcend
burrows underneath the Sky's edge.
All the black beetles on the California desert
and all the great blue whales
are real people.

The buckeye butterfly is lovely as a condor.
Hawks migrate above our houses.

Circles of light move over concrete.
Our caves stay open
behind changing faces.
Flames flow
like incandescent
syrup
—heaped up in
waves
and
breakers—
all across the landscape.

Some days
the air
is gray fire.

Brown air
makes bizarre
sunsets.

AURAS

hang

in new

places!

Behind doors
and
over engines.

OLD RADIANCES
begin
to disappear.

Where is the foxfire
in
Jack O'Lantern time?

When will Mr. Frost doodle on the window
with his nippy hands?

NOW WITH MY HANDS UPON THE GEARS
WE ZOOM OUT . . .

JEALOUS OF A WOLF!
I am a monster. You are a monster.
YOU
can be loved
and cuddled like a chick.

Peeping in our incubators.
Stirring in the chrysalis is what we're told
we're doing.
IRISH ELKS SWIMMING THROUGH A SEWER
THAT RUNS BENEATH A CRUMBLING CITY.

Jays perch outside the window—staring in
and laughing.
The horsehair snake makes a shadow in the sun.
He is coppery—a thick wire. He has no mouth
except a groove. He grew in the body
of a cricket—living on the juices in the muscle.
Then he burrowed out through the cricket's shell.
Now warm water is his home. He is a cave
with no eye holes—but he is all sense.
Mosquito larvae dash
from the area of disturbance—where
he makes a tiny cloud of turbulence
from particles of soft gray
and velvety sediment.
The huge furry creature who has been drinking
raises up his head The cattails
rattle slightly
in
the
wind.

THEY
SAID
THERE IS A SILVER LIGHT
behind all things and that bodies
are the masks we change—as one
might blink his eyes
after a drizzle as he stands in a graveyard
surrounded by a field of rainbows.

And the larvae love the sun and oxygen
and
they
know
all things
around them
move.

THE PREDATORS MAKE PATTERNS IN THE AIR.
Wolf and coyote are oscilloscopes.
The last red wolves are in thickets
to the south.

Mozart playing with the universe.
Boccherini thinking timeless thoughts while mission padres
eliminate the Indians
and put their souls
in pearly boxes.
Ants
celebrating rites
of blackness
in the sweetened air.

ARCHWAYS WHERE THE SUN STREAMS IN!

BOLTS OF LIGHTNING FROZEN IN THE AIR!

SHEWANNAH IN THE SHAPE OF BUFFALO POURING
THROUGH YOUR EAR!

April kissing August in a cave.

The edge lifts up like a lip.
Then it all becomes a sail of finest stuff
—gray French velvet
tinged with pink
embroidered
by
the thought
we hurl toward
it.
And it grows
our mother's face
and smiles

at us
AS
we
always
knew
it would.
Then she says
in kind words
(so sensitive)
that she is roaring
at us
if we would hear her.
She says that she is stroking
us
if we
would remember.

GREEN SEA LETTUCE IN THE TIDE POOLS.

"YOU'RE JUST A BABY IN DISGUISE."

·

"AHA! I AM NOT SURPRISED.
A VAST CAVERN CARVED
OUT OF THE ICE!"

·

And then gray turbulence drifts past a bubble in the mud.
The sun shines back to itself from the water's skin
like a silver tiger leaping all ways at once.
Cattails make dark green shadows.
The image of an osprey in the distance dives
through a ripple.
The sound of a nearby splash.
Slushing suction of huge hairy foot
in mud.
He is as large as a truck.
He bends his head to drink from the shining
water.
Mosquito
larvae
plunge
and
dance
like drunken sirens.

THE SALMON GRABS THE MAYFLY!

*You are tired of being
someone else?*

THE WORLD
we stand in
is an aura
THAT
WE
SHAPE

AROUND
US.

All our trails
in it
are
our
last
illusion.

AHA! I AM NOT SURPRISED.
A VAST CAVERN CARVED
OUT OF THE ICE!

YOU'RE JUST A BABY IN DISGUISE!

The first is where the last is once again!

THE GAME IS REAL AS GOLDEN DAYS AND POLYMERS.
Billiard balls in heaven bounce off Pythagoras.
YELLOW FLASHES!
(Clicks of light.)
Garter snakes speeding on green velvet.
Neuron
ripples
catch the drift
of fresh surprise.
LUCK
is
made this way
—and emanates the silhouettes
of vanity at worst.
At best we are reborn each instant
every day
into eternity.
((OR
SOME
OTHER
DELUSION.))

IT IS BEST TO BE HERE AS WE DIVE THROUGH SPACE.
Feel ourselves as the muscles
stretch to make us.
THIS IS TRULY ALCHEMY!

THIS   THIS
IS   IS THE
TRULY   SECRET
ALCHEMY!   BOOK!
And   And
there   there
are   are

STARS
IN

GROANING
BOXES.
Bearded smiles.
Drops of gleaming wax on parchment.
Crickets playing host to gods.
Smells of fresh-cut wood.
A figure dancing with a sword.
Men with deer horns.
Breasts on eagles.
Smoke in mist.
Rivers rippling.

Honest lovers' grins.

Beauteous girls in minuet.

SPEAK, OH RAVENS BLOOD!

"WE LOVE THE BODY. WE WISH TO HOLD IT.
THE BODY IS A STONE.
The rock is a body.
The boulder cares.
The gravel stares
with gravity sensors
from underneath
the lithic lid.
WE RUSH TO HUG AND CRUSH AND KISS
THE PRECIOUS THING
that grins at us referring back
itself as homunculus
of what we are.
We do not stare closely. Almost anything
of flesh will do
whether it has scaly tail
or violet wings
or barks or mews.
WE NEED THE MORPHOS AND THE NEWS
it brings us.
It does not fill us with cold rhyme
but with huge warm love
that is nearly
the kind of thing
that Luck is."

WE GRAB THE LOVELY THING AND SPEAK TO IT AS IF
WE WERE A BABY!
The secret language is unveiled.
We always knew it
but
forgot to speak.
AS
WE KISS IT

it becomes an egg
again. A fantastic
sleek, smooth thing
in a bag of water
staring out.
A perfect form
with no rough edges

smoothed over

in the riverbed

of what someone calls

TIME.

(Lying on scarlet silk sheets.)

OR IN A MULTICOLORED GROTTO . . .
With prints of flowers
that pass through minds of Byzantium
and Han.
Pictures and poems pop from the walls.
Veils of fog drift through the street
and hang outside the casement
where Arabs tamper with plastique.

THERE IS A BLUEBIRD FLYING IN THE STONE.

A lion dances on the apricots.

The body shows it is a cloud
by being solid.

Coffee grinders make spinnerets of sound.
A saber slashes through a brow
and the tree shrew
does somersaults
chasing tiny rodents.

THERE!

THERE!

THERE YOU ARE AGAIN!
I have been pursuing tendrils.
We are topologies of cells
and distribution patterns
reduced down

from our projections.
We are auras of visages
that
sing
around
the serpent's tongue.
WE ARE THE VISION
THAT WE'RE SCARED
TO HAVE!
AND HERE WE STAND
with
TOES
and
EARS
like Li'l Abner
or the sacred Khan.

Dancing in the wildwood once again.

WE ARE STICK FIGURES CARVED ON CLIFFS OF STARS
(with swirlings round our heads
that draw us into flesh).
The cash
we pay for things
is the cost of every word.
There are herds
of shaggy beings
in the opal.
One furry thing stands
in the oaky delta where the water runs
in streams. Where the sun beats down
upon cattails. He scratches
at the water's surface with his giant claws.
He looks up with deep-set eyes and sees
the fish hawk.
In the meadow
far behind
are carnivores with snouts.
Long-necked beings stand on the horizon.
The osprey hovers with wings upthrust
and tremulous. The fairy tale
of lives begins
and ends
at any point.

Fingers stretch across space
while ships
flash back
and
forth.

The flowered men cry out
like Crazy Horse.

THE SEA PALMS NEED THE SURGE.

Gray mariposa lilies/
furred kitten paws.

Huge mussels.

Rhododendrons in the forest.

Touches on the shoulder.

Girls in tuxedos dance with canes.

Collaborators throwing kisses to their brains.

Sharks' teeth.

HAZELNUTS STRETCHING INTO THOUGHTS.

THE FAIRY RADIANCES THAT HANG IN AIR
ARE SHIELDS ABOUT OUR HEADS.
The floating
falling
leaves
are just
the same.
Your name
is writ
in fair
scratches
and the billowings
of golden dust.
The bedstead and the distant mount
(beneath the radar cones)
and the fireplace
in between
are planes
that fools
and sages
see as
stained glass
peepholes
to
an
other scene.

ALL

THE

OUTRÉ

TELLS

ME

that the universes are
a tear-off jacket of tattoos
all sleeveless
and draped across my shoulders
with coconuts for buttons
and a tarantula for boutonniere!
I
have wings,
and antlers,
hairy legs,
horse's ears,
a giant pizzle,
a drunken father,
AND
A
MORTAR LAUNCHER
FOR A BOW.

YOU WILL KNOW ME BY THE STORIES THAT I TELL!

YOU
WILL
EVEN
KNOW
THAT
WE
ARE
LOVELY
COLTS
STUMBLING
IN
our
first
snow
and leaving prints all over white December
and
tiny ferns
in shadows of big rocks
and scented barns
in empty fields
with
doves
nesting
in
the haylofts
—and a slowly running stream
where catfish dream.

AND SO WE STRETCH OUT
to the white truck
that parks beside the curb
by the universe
near the grotto.
IN

                        THE
                      SECTOR
            WHERE REAL VISIONS PLAY
                 ALL OVER CLIFFS.
            And the walls clutch themselves
          and hug into a capsule like a ball
                  but they unroll
                 when we stroll
                       by.
                        I
                 whistle casually
              as if I do not know.

  I KNOW HOW ALL THINGS WORK AND I AM PLEASED.
            I MAKE GREAT BOATS
          from cardboard tubes of Quaker Oats
                and nails and string
                and rubber bands.
          To build a crystal palace for the princess
                   is my game.

   My pretty kitten is the champion boxer of the fairy tales.

AND FINALLY
REACHING
IN
THE
CAVE
(or out of it)
THERE IS NOTHING
THAT CAN BE TAKEN SERIOUSLY
OR NOT
and there is no size,
big or small,
that can be measured
on a scale.
We can never smell or taste enough of it.
The walls are marshmallow
covered with chrome
and changed to flesh.
The color of a plum
reflecting back
the seriousness of a forest.
IT
IS
A
FLAME
and a fairy radiance!

Everything increases as it crumples
back upon itself. It gathers
strength
that way
to make
a leap that may
or may not happen.
I RIDE MY WHITE CAMEL—OR MY TRUCK—
ACROSS THE FLAMING DESERT
with the moon behind my turban,

chanting songs
of childhood
that
happen
in the future.
CARPETS OF LONG-LEGGED KING CRABS
crawl across the ocean's icy floor.

Kinky hairs float in sunny wind.

Autos honk in tunnels.

Chocolate kisses wrapped in shining foil.

((((ONCE AGAIN I HAVE REASON TO BELIEVE IN
ALL THE CLOUDS
that make these puffs
of clouds.
I know that they are wrapped
around one another
and wove together
to make a shapeless
Uncarved Block.

WHEN ALL THE PIECES
draw back
there is then the nothing
left behind.
))))

Spots of red fruit
squashed on white clapboard.

Fossil fish
that swim through slate.

Date palms by the oasis.
Lonely tigers growling in their sleep.

St. Francis dancing with the Areopagite
while Plato and Lao Tsu
roar with laughter.

Pink mattresses stacked one thousand high.
Conveyor belts of buckets filled with nectar.

Lobsters cooking.

Cord convertibles
that nap in front of art deco buildings.

Glaciers moving towards
the Kansas seabed.
EVERYTHING
all
caught up together
like the beings in a submarine
—and watching

while they writhe and kiss

with silk-gloved hands

and
turn on the projector for the final movie.

(Call that the Steamship Universe.)

BECAUSE IT IS THE ULTIMATE IN BEAUTY
(and the ONLY)
the many Selves
of us touch it
as we slide by
OR
AS
IT
PASSES
OVER US!

ONLY IN OUR ARROGANCE DO WE ASK FOR
SIMPLICITY AND SHININESS!
It does not gleam except when we distort it.
Then it is like an ancient movie shown
too many times.
All the scratches wear away the nose and eyes
and elbows.
Blurred forms
perform vaguely sexy
duties.
The projectionist
says that this
is either art or pornography.
The sensation pleases
but
outside

(in the explosion)

there is wet fog and the crunch
of autumn leaves.
The sounds of car crashes.
Fire trucks whooping.
Facets in the air like crystal candy.

OLD
MEN
singing to the spirit of the tiger.

Wolves in dens on hillsides.

AWAKENING IN PAINLESS YOUTH AGAIN
but knowing
it is painless youth.

FREE OF ALL DESIRES TO BE A *THING.*

Aware that the mind will not liberate.

On hands and knees chewing on the luscious grass tufts,
clouds in shapes of sages drifting overhead.

THE
SELVES
PRINT
THEM
SELVES:

CAVE
MOUTH
WITH
A
HALO

WINGED
HANDS

FINGERS
WITH
STINGERS
OF
BEES

WASPS
SLEEPING
UNDER
TREES

((Picture-bubble:
a huge beast
drinking from a pond
then killed
by men.))

MARBLE
COOLING
IN
A

MULTICOLORED
PUDDLE

A
HERO
CHOKING
DRAGONS
ON
A
CLIFF

BLUE
MACAWS
DRYING
WET
FEATHERS
IN
THE
SUN

THE ISLE OF OKINAWA IN A MISTY SEA—A PUFF OF ROCKY TURBULENCE.

TUESDAY.

FRIDAY.

Drinking wine from tiny cups.
Anemones that tremble in the wind.

White hibiscus growing on the riverbank.

Desert poppies on a gray-green bush.

The buildings disappear and tall ones rise
and make excitement.
I can
feel the change
about me. Thrill
comes charging through
the skin. The
air roars silently
over many years.
We
gather
it
as
we
walk
by
and grin.

This Power distills ennui into an intoxicant.

THIS AXE SHINES.

A hand hangs there in space.

The air is a living cloth of sounds.

The fall and rising of the buildings
leaves a charge
in space.
It
is all another bubble
on the ripple's edge.

The escalator floats me
to the wave.

A<small>ND SO I RISE</small>
TO
WHERE
THE
EAGLES WHEEL
IN SQUADRONS!

AND
SO
I
pass
by
the
ivory
statuette
of
reality!

The speeding spaceships hang forever steadily
immobile.
Men make guttural shouts and swing their swords.
Slashing
through the brow.
Circles of light play upon the concrete walls.

We hold it in our palms
and crush and kiss
it
all at once.

I TELL YOU THIS IS BEAUTY!

YOU TELL ME THIS IS BEAUTY!

We
ache as if we're smashed

by parts of us.

WE WISH TO BELIEVE.

OUR
DISBELIEF
IS
PAIN.

WE'RE STRETCHED
—STRUNG-OUT LIKE BUBBLE GUM!

EVERYTHING WE'RE SUPPOSED TO KNOW
GRABS OUT AT US:
social loves,
Chevrolets
and *Boccherini!*

———————————————

We sail right on past—free as sunfish!

BUT
WITH THE STEADY ACHE
THAT KNOWLEDGE CARVES IN US
WHERE CAN WE GO?

Why,
to where we are.

I hold this ivory statuette for you to look at.
It is a carving of you showing something to me.

A
HERO
CHOKING
DRAGONS
ON
A
CLIFF.

Eagle squadrons swirling into stars.

A chariot of hungers all alive with shining eyes.

Starlings squeaking on the rooftops.
A billion points of light.
Black holes catching photons.

Unknown thoughts
(true
muscular
sensations)
going to a masquerade
in strange costumes.
While everything pours outward—steadily and faster!

TILL

WE
GUESS
THAT
Paradise
IS
SMOKE
ABOVE THE FIRE

AND
I
grin

relieved
at
last!

I LOVE YOUR EYES!

DO YOU LOVE MINE?

A
HERO
CHOKING
DRAGONS
ON
A
CLIFF

★

A
HERO
CHOKING
DRAGONS
ON
A
CLIFF

★

Blue
macaws . . .

AND SO WE STRETCH OUT . . .
All explosions at the Battle
of Okinawa
or
the
Universe's
core
are
nothing

compared to this shape
I feel
of what I want
but cannot name.

I
prove, by the way things
break me up,
that there is no measure.
I am permanent in change
and all uncarved.

WE FLOAT ALONG.
We are the laughing crest upon the whitecap.

The walls of the cathedral
flood their images. They say

we're going ninety million miles per hour.

The osprey's picture dives across the pond between the cattails.

PUSSYWILLOWS OPEN HERE IN OCTOBER'S IDES!

Water strider shadows break up.
Huge claws jar the water's surface,
making lines of light on bottom
in the brilliant sun.
The monster's deep-set eyes look at the sky.
Branches of creosote hang from the mouth as he drinks.
The coppery horsehair snake writhes by . . .
Mosquito larvae dive. The painted men
almost giggle
in the rushes.
The sound of water being swallowed in a giant throat.
One man with ochred face and scarlet
eyeholes raises up his
leaf-shaped sword of flint
and kisses it.
He sees
the color that he is
reflected there.
The man with green stripes
trembles sexually
and thinks of blood.
He holds the magic club encrusted with the teeth
and carved with faces.
The tufts of feathers on it drink
flesh juice.
Ochre Head stands
and raises up the flint.

Green Stripes rushes forward with a gleeful scream!
Three snouted creatures in the field beyond the oak trees
raise their heads and peer.

Vultures cock their eyes.

The horsehair snake wriggles in the warm pond water.

The theater we know
is the edges
of our organs,
and
our
selves
are actors.

—Falling through the walls.

HEADS
POKING
DOWN
FROM CEILINGS
—giggling.

THE
POLLYWOG
POND
is
at
the cliff base.
Petrified bones of dinosaurs
hang out above
the tadpoles.
WE
TURN
INTO
TITANS

that
swoop

back
to

our
roots.

We
wear

red
capes

and
sail

through
space.

I
leave
splashes
of
my radiance

adrift
in
everywhere.

Monsters
flee
my
swordpoint.

The white buildings

swoop
upward.

These are my shining scales.

My
BODY

turns
the many

colors
that

I
know

it
is

and
I

enjoy it!

This
is

where
I

guess
what

shapes

I

grow
to.

Here
I
am
in
a
pocket
grotto
with
all
pressure
turned
inward
to
me.

It
is

not
pain.

HERE
IS

the bison hunt.

Here
are

war
whoops.

now
is

the
city

on
the

cliff
top.

Here
are
control
switches
miniaturized.

Now
I

choose
to

grow

an

arm
or
leg
or to
be
a
Lucifer
or
friendly ghost
of
self

or
a
love
god.

Touch here or *press* there.

BUT LOVE BURSTS!

TO BE A MAN
IS TO BE A MAMMAL-MAN
WITH STYLE
that
does not matter
since all lives are forgotten
when we dissolve in black sugar.
The stately form we had in mind
becomes a turbulence. We learn
that our thoughts
are tiny mountains
and the roots of trees
that we sleep within
stretch through
stellar space.

AND LOVE BURSTS AND THE CREATURE
HULKING OVER US SCREECHES, WHISTLING AIR,
AND PUKES UP WATER, STOPS,
STARES AT US IN WONDER ALMOST HYPNOTIZED
with his own love.
Huge dumb furry face—and giant claws
making magic gestures in the air!
I know he knows that he is dying!
I
WARD THE MAGIC OFF
WITH A THOUGHT!
He bares his chest
and I leap up with the flint sword!
My face is ochre.
His
shit
pours

into
the
pond.
His red blood dissolves the osprey's picture
in the waves.

AND I BREAK OUT AND CRY IN LONG-
FORGOTTEN SONGS!

HE STANDS WITH THE FLINT STUCK IN HIM.

HE IS I—AND I AM HIM.
WE ARE THE RIVER POURING TO THE ROOTS
THAT FEED THE BLOSSOM!

WE ARE THE RIVER!

WE ARE THE RIVER!

OUR FACES ARE THE WAVES!

AFTERWORD: FROM A CONVERSATION

HARALD MESCH: In *Rare Angel* there seems to be a significant interplay between the—as far as I can see—synonymous terms "curb," "edge," and "on the precipice." Did you intend any relationship among them?

MICHAEL MCCLURE: I was unaware of it, but there probably is.

MESCH: You couldn't comment on that?

MCCLURE: The whole poem is about being on the edge.

MESCH: What do you understand by "being on the edge"?

MCCLURE: Being on the edge of the explosion.

MESCH: Of the ecological catastrophe?

MCCLURE: It is happening right now. We all thought that the world is going to blow up, and it is; we didn't realize how slowly it was going to blow up. We're looking at an explosion happening in slow motion. Resources are being turned into cinders and gases, and forests are being turned into cinderlike structures of buildings, riverbeds are being blown up into freeways. Imagine the world a hundred years ago and a hundred years in the future.

MESCH: You speak of the danger of the "brink" or of the "edge" we are on. At the same time you're saying that we're in love with this danger. Since we love it, we obviously look for it, provoke it. We obviously enlarge and enhance that danger—isn't that a contradiction?

MCCLURE: I don't know that it is a contradiction. I want people to be aware, though, that it is *our primate nature* to enjoy what we're doing.

MESCH: Even if we're burning up gas and polluting the biosphere, even if we are exploding the substrata of our being?

MCCLURE: Yes, and if we realize how much we really enjoy it and why we enjoy it and what a great thrill it is and . . .

MESCH: But it might be stupid, too.

MCCLURE: Clearly. But it is too easy to say it is stupid. We can't self-righteously tell other people who are enjoying it, when we are in the process of enjoying it ourselves, that it is simply stupid, that they are fools. So, one thing we can do is make people understand how beautiful it is and that it is our nature to do those things and that they are beautiful *and* they are stupid at the same time for us and for the future and for all life. . . .

MESCH: It's not necessarily our nature, is it? I mean, the Indians didn't do it.

MCCLURE: The Indians were destructive in their own ways. That is why I often talk about Paul Martin's idea [in *Pleistocene Extinctions*] that it was probably the ancestors of the Indians, the Paleo-Indians, who wiped out twenty-six genera of megafauna, the upper tier of the Pleistocene megafauna, in the New World when they entered it—everything from the wild horse to the ground sloths. This is called the Overkill Hypothesis. They destroyed everything from the mastodons to the forest bison. If we understand that, then we say: "Oh, that's what we love to do, that's what we like to do, we like to do that. We love to kill big animals." But then we say, "But if we like to do that, if we go any further, then we are not going to have any mammal brethren left." But first of all, you can't righteously take a stance that this *is* evil, this is not human. This is, in fact, entirely human, this is our nature. Then we say, "Ah, but our nature has *other* possibilities." If we acknowledge that this is our nature, what *other* possibilities does our nature have? What else could we do that is natural? That's the crucial thing that I can see. Yes, I think it has to be stopped right away, but I think it must be stopped by saying: "Oh, *that's* who we are. I get it! I see! I understand. That's me."

MESCH: You are saying: "Politics is dead—Biology is here . . ." Biology, i.e., the revolt of our bodies, or with our bodies? How would you describe that revolt as it may take place in everyday life?

McCLURE: There is a wonderful young man in California. He was concerned about a river that was about to be dammed, a wild river which would be dammed for the sheer fucking purpose of sending water to southern California, water that they didn't need. The young man announced to the newspapers and to all the media that he was going to chain himself to a rock in the bottom of the canyon that would be filled if they dammed the river. And he went down and chained himself to a rock where no one could find him, and they didn't dam the river.

MESCH: I fully agree with such acts.

McCLURE: That's biology.

DARK
BROWN *(1961)*

the struggle to it is DARK BROWN the struggle
itself is a solid moving in an inferno . . .

OH GIDDY BLANK WHITE PAGE OH DREAMY MAN
OH INTERRED SPIRIT BULK
in meat and hand. Oh both
are one! Oh love black white and dream Rose and Purple,
and green and scratched. Oh sleeping Lion,
man. Oh beast. Oh Black
ODEM. OH

Depth within. Oh limited void, as far
as eyes can see and nose can smell. Oh dreamer.
OH PRIDE GOD SHIT AND ACHING STRETCH RIB. NO NOT

Lion not the shit of metaphor. The deep and
singing beast! Void instead! OH

---

crap upon the page.

I dream and walk in my dream with proud stride. I am clean
and dream with brown eye. I am free
OF LIBERTY.

THE BODY THE SPIRIT ARE ONE I AM
energy!

' am muscled space. Am meat
and colored light.
ROMANTIC CRY

ONLY MAN GOD I SHIT LOVE BEAST ODEM
I CALL FROM DARKNESS TO BONEWHITE
space, by means of nerve and tendon   speak / sing / thru

the space. The space crossed by muscled
energy.

Or say—a drift.
Of music, real heedless,
WHINING UNCARING BITTER REJOICING HUNGRY
for Triumph, lip
smacking! OH!
And never, never chained.
AND HUGE FREEING THE MAN TO WHAT IS NOBLE
TO THE CLOUD MOVING
change he wrecks on what is about in the tiny the huge void
the room and Milky Way about him. Tossing his protein,
wrestling my / I / my meat, throwing myself about in light
listening. To the heard singer in the pit in the pool.
The relentless bad rhymer. Sawing his ceaseless violin
flapping and clanking his appendages!
MOVING THE SEEKING HUGE AND BEAUTIFUL
MAMMALED SHAPE
around and driving him to deeds.
Moving him real thru clouds he disgorges. Lighting
his / my / brown eyes with

Fire??

So shall you blame those
who give it up, those who say
it isn't worth the struggle?
—Olson

YES I BLAME THEM IN THEIR GODDAMNED WEAKNESS OF
THEIR FEAR OF BLOOD
those who walk softly crumpled in their fear of the
cold. Who gather smoke to obfuscate the void. Forgetting it is smoke

—and gather smoke not honey. I Blame
them. This is not the easy
Damnation that I want but Hell. I have
been undamned for days. Sick without sickness,

I blame weakness, I put down the final search
for pleasure. I cry that all is cold
and after that I hope to act.
To stride easily in my inhabited
void.
!WANT NOTHING NEVERMORE WITH EASE!

Oh WHY OH WHY THE BLASTED LOVE
THE HUGE SHAPE CHANGE ? OH WHY
the tortured hand when clouds are down? I love
your lips and hands and legs. Your backbone line,
your breasts. The movement of your face and move
from them now. Oh why the words of lies above. Oh why the shape
change of movement, energy? when I will return to you
Oh awkward Love awkward, I love your
fingertips. Oh black
and sorrowed night. Oh mother and child.
Must I learn new love anew. No
choice! Are we joined forever
or is that lies! I remember
love in darkness and feel of flesh. Oh
CHANGE

No ease to truth. I half admit it.

ENVY FALSEHOOD DECEIT BUT LARKSPUR DARK
IN THE LIGHT

(Where

the skullback moth sleeps aday.) Larkspur phantom
gray and black in the memory. What are the colors, russet,
red and blue? How long since the child / I / have
seen you. Knowing the larkspur stands
The phantom strong in my mind! But larkspur

dark in the light. Now envy falsehood deceit

and black I raise from it. Like
the larkspur. Oh phantom ever in my body

LARKSPUR IN MY ARMS LEGS AND CHEST.

AND EVER RISE OUT OF IT ALSO FROM THE IMAGE
IMAGO THE CHILD

OH EASE OH BODY-STRAIN OH LOVE OH EASE ME NOT!
WOUND-BORE
be real, show organs, show blood, OH let me
be as a flower. Let ugliness arise without care
grow side by side with beauty. Oh twist
be real to me. Fly smoke! Meat-real, as nerves
TENDON
Ion, FLAME, Muscle, not banners but bulks as
we are all "deer"
and move as beasts. Stalking in our forest
as these are speech-words!

Burn them pure as above they rise from attitude are
stultified. Are shit. Burn
what arises from habit. Let custom
die. Smash patterns and forms let spirit
free to blasting liberty. Smash the
habit shit above ! ! ! ! ! ! ! ! !

LET PURE BLACK WORDS MOVE FROM THOUGHT BEHIND

NOTHING I AM BUT I MOVE, NOTHING I AM BUT I MAKE

not that dull thing but that I disperse smoke, and build
what I want. And match my love in a dark
brown mirror. And seek desire in a similar
eye.   OH fake of vanity
the shapes are many. Habit and
custom are ease are ease. EASE

no truth with ease. The child
rises up. To say / oh ache to see
the simple / good and bad, chained and
liberty. And oh the huge and simpleness
of what he means. OH

AND THE GREAT CLEAR AIR OF ALL HIS MOTIONS

AND THE PROPORTIONLESSNESS OF ALL HE SEES

THE SUN BEING A STAR TO HIM

THE ROOT THE ION THE PRIDE TO THE LEAF THE BLOOD
AND ORGANS
to the Beast. OH BLOOD OH CRY SHIT GOD CHRIST

THE SHOUT AND SLAM OF FOOT IN THE HOLLOW ROOM

THE WINDING OF MUSIC WITHIN IT

Not music but the sound of what is felt. Sound
made by the interior. (The words are small
I fail.) The Romantic cry
and structure. Blake's invention. The
SOUND the TORCH
in the dark cave, this last note.
The thing made and heard by the beast, the pride
of the flower. The pride of the ion?
That this is all a whole in a greater space
and matters more. And goes on

NO! I RELENT TO EASE

A last final failure again. My triumph.
The pride of my shape. The pride of my love. The pride
of myself. The pride of my child. The pride
of my pride. The pride of my loud foot typing hands and
hair. That I
broaden that I will not give surcease
save that I rest that my motions will be
stronger.   !

THE GREAT LONG DAMNED AND UNDAMNING / thing / PATH

THE CLOUDLESS CLEAR AND BLACK

AN IMAGE: THE BLAST HURLS RED AND FLAMING BRANDS
AND THE BRANDS
hurl brands as they descend. As they fall each
gathering oxygen to itself spurting and blazing

casting flaming knots of itself from itself,
becoming huger. Or a cascade
of water the same. Caught in the light

the brown and blueblack salmon
moving against it . . .

The brands hurling brands making a dome
in descent. No moral, no Love—
. . . words . . .

BUT THE BURNING GODDAMNED THING WITHIN
IS CALM / TENSE
and energetic. Forces itself upon itself
without contradiction. Has no symmetry but
the symmetry of shape! No
plan.

No plan, but Hunger, Desire.
And love of body. Love.

THE *AELF-SCIN*, THE SHINING *SCIMMER* THE GLEAM, THE
SHINING
color of walls of scratches of cracks of brightness
the cold mystery the (Philip calls it) Weir. The *déjà*
vu of the forest-sorrel, tiny, leaves sun-folded
bent like a head in uniqueness. Animal in look
to fold so. The moment I
leave what I am in *aelf-scin*. Stand
in wonder. Lose myself. Even to fear.
A difference. *Aelf-scin*, Weir. But
similar. Knowing its name the horror
of void is gone. Knowing it almost
with my ash spear over my arm in the black
FOREST CLEAR WATER AND AIR SEA

The Anglo-Saxons build huge boats fight battles
and rejoice in what they see,
see beauty more clearly
have words for what
I forget. Live in
libery. For
ever. ! ! ! !

CALL IT FEAR NOW-GONE
the whole thing a star
breathing.

YES OH BLASTED MAN I OH ACHE OF LOVE HULK OF
ARTERIES AND VEINS
red light thru windowed eyelids. To what is black
and wet within. To genes directing arm and leg

to the unknown bulk that never pauses
in my move. But blocked. Blocked, that
blasts
flowing and billowing from the gut. Stop
turning me, oh ache oh move. I break
THRU THRU THRU THRU THRU the size of any
STAR!
Alive as a plant or any star.
RAPTOR OF MY OWN DESIRES
not winged but armed for freedom.
Bright as my own eye or muscle. (Each
chemical exchange no larger than
a nova) Oh dullness of mind,
sharpen the body. Not the easy
thing or word. Guard me that I speak
truth. Love me for my sight
of me. Never bless or love me,
call on me for action. Speak
not without moving what is you. Move
not air alone. Oh dullness. Breathe
brightness of inferno heat. Blaze
clear flames that do not dazzle. Strike
down what lies already. Open

CLEAR AS AN IRIS OR MACKEREL.

BREATHE BRIGHT FUCKING AIR ! ! !

STAR!

CHILD ! !

IMAGE

((OH BRING OH BLOOD BACK THE COURAGE THE DEEP
THE NEGATIVE CHALLENGE
I deny. Love. Deny. Defy oh love. In blackness
a forest, oh damp earth. Put forth. Decry! Put down
until a shoot is sent forth matching. The purity
the image within. Oh crass and easy polemic

say:
! I LOVE !
Let me be a torch to myself.))
OH HEART-SICK BURN STRIVE Past the drift-ease
to the depth within making a film of the gene
over the surface. *Say* meat hand, the hand black
in the deed as the strain toward the act. Each strike
an ugly huge music. Walking walking huge Love.

All a web from the black gene to the black
edge.
(((torture destroy tradition seek what gives damned
pleasure.)))
Exult in drugs
draw back to sight,
VISION
of purity & liberty.
MORTALITY IS BEAUTY THE BEAST SPIRIT LIVES FOREVER
!   !

!

I REST

THE BLACK BLACK BLACK DAMNED AND UNDREAMY
ODEM THE UNDERSOUL

the shit shaped dark light. The Gene.
Maker of love for love. Everlasting real opposite
of solid real. Most vacuous in the hole
that matter is. Contemptuous self-loving
darkness. Crying No death, no death, no death,
without fear! Alive
forever.
TORCH! TORCH! TORCH!
in the light night. Unclouded one.
Undersoul. Odem, Dark brown, Umber, Beast.
The undersoul a star!
BREATH PLASMA BLACK ROARER
enchained,
and whining humorist. Oh
energy and cloudless motion. I

remember again the sharp loving.
There is no death for heroes! !

This / a dumb ode.
I remember hands in the night (mine yours) and huge joy   past,
not ease, thinking it was dead, and now know it goes,
on, without, I am now, you are now, there is no cease.
No need to remember me, I remember you. On,
on.

DESTROY DESTROY DESTROY
Create and
never cease. Oh

build
grand loving arms.

ABAVED DEARN A-DEARN DEATH-FEAR WHY Are you here??

OH BRIGHT MAN WHY FLAME-FEAR WHEN YOU ARE BLACK
and dive into blackness. Into the swart
dark-brownness and now live in fires. Apitch

tuned and sent rushing, impeded
tossed back, channeled, rifted, serried
TEDIUM
I mean become a stream rushing, branches
waving. Sent in fear. Regretting. Tossed
by anothers face and
hand. Why
OH GOD FUCK SWEET BREATH RUSHING SHIT DO I

REPEAT LOVE REPEAT?
Confused by the confusion. I Beast
am star. Am same as star. Call on sweet-
ness to be not sweet. Enroil what I contain
in the tube of me. Breathe. Pneumas.
Call of oh stark. I
STRETCH RAISE RISE PUT FORTH AS

AN IRIS. MY BLOOD MY BREATH

DEEP-DELVE

refuse fuck to sing. Oh. OH.

Hate the silly fucking image.

PROFANE. PROFANE.

!

OH PROPORTIONLESS OH SCREAM CRY RISE BACK UP
OUT

LIVE IN HELL TAILED DREAM-FREED OF EASE.

SEE CLEAR SAY DIE. OH EDGED FACE OF BEAUTY
black and white in gloaming. Oh face bent to the
child silhouette.
STRANGE SHAPES OF LOVE STRANGE SHAPES OF LOVE
dream of me often. I fight,
watch bend you delving, loose, oh love
strange shapes of the love, struggle,
shapes of struggle. Stir in darkness
HALF-LIGHT. WILL
fight forever for your love. Fight
ease-ache, ease-lust, refuse
to love at all dream, change.

Except the black unchanging gene.
&
ORGAN MUSCLED MAMMAL.

OH STRONG STRONG STRONG IN MY STUPID
weakness.
Spread forever.

Oh deep oh sorrow blood beast bag eye-skinned
FREE ME, GUT!

I am free, am liberty, moved tossed by the sight
VISION
by my, I am Star am beast, am even
with the great striving hand. Motion, moving
the air. Not a cloud but a gesture, not
smoke maker, burning black from the beast within,
the clean flame. Ready to cry, lament,
sing elegies and damn
them. No myth. No myth no myth

BUT A DECLAMATION! !

My edge-cliff song. My heart-love book.

TRAP! !

Voice itself, small words. Spirit, Hugeness.

Odem not Geist. Odem

STRIP THE UNCLEAN.

Danger! !

OH BRIGHT OH BLACK SINGBEAST LOVEBEAST
CATKIN SLEEK
spined and gullet shaped. Free me

in the tree-lighted evening and full cool
morning. OH
VISION free me erect and huge to VISION

DEEP-DELVED

OUTDELVING. BANNER-
hung and warm warmly gestured
star gestured in
the coldness.
Fingers spread pointing.

The only vision sight-sense.

OH CHRIST OH DEATH GOD FUCKING SHIT DIVE ME
oh sing sight see Romantic Cry

Free to say I love, I hate, in bat-light.
YOUR WARM HAND
THE BREATH OF YOUR GUT
Your thigh and tooth.
Your sight of me.
Oh Rose Rose Rose, oh Spiritual hunt, oh glossy
bleeding, multicolored, single
bright star.

SERAPH I, CRY
down above my cloud. My precipice,
my black and bloody bonehall, love littered
day cot. Chalice seeker. Rose
love / hater. Deceit and uneasiness!

Seraph I, unlaugher to laugh. Spring
to your burrow
in weakness!

& make not shapes I love that tense
to freedom.

O ache oh ache-ode.

GLORIA! GLORIA! GLORIA! NERVE ARTERY TORCH I AM.
Freed of politics. Stand brightly. Build
anti-venom. Stave off love build
new love from hatred. Twist in the new
chair.
NO! NEW EYES. MAKE NEW EYES TO SEE THAT I AM SERAPH

EXACTLY WHAT I AM. UNEVENESS
of spirit. Love-flame dreamer

damning love. Begging and refusing
figure 8-ing
LOVE ME, I CRY, LOVE ME
And swell to my size. Each moment
eternal, each anew. Nothing is lost, I try

moving to it. To love. Begging forgiveness,
FORGETTING THE MOMENT

passes. The moment
passes and the moment passes. I Seraph
forget that I am free. Make
motions. All is past. The flame
is bright again. Speak clear.
OH GLORIA GLORIA GLORIA GLORIA GLORIA
of strength. And you before me.
Love-dream builder I make it with
nothing but words. Oh what can

WE USE BUT OUR ACTIONS??
What are words? Acts I

make to you without image
metaphor. Bare fact.
Strives to be truth. Simplicity
and nothing more. I ask

you for nothing.
Give!
BASE LIE.
Never, never give me nothing!
Let me writhe till I act to you.
OH COLDNESS.

BUT MORE THAT I AM MAMMAL AM GOD DENY-ER
AM ATHEIST
one breathing star sized. Oh Odem-spirit! free
OH SHIT BLOCKED HUNGERER

I WILL NOT GIVE YOU BEAUTY! There
is but one beauty. Without proportion

all containing,
containing exclusions,

it is hideous, too good
for you. Sorrow is Sorrow

HUNGER IS HUNGER. There are lies
to block all truth. Close your ears
to others. Brighten the protein coil.
Oh only, only once forever. This is the last
chance. And then no other. And one more.
OH BLEED GIVE STRENGTH TO BLOOD.
FOLLOW
not the rivulets, clear bright streams

tossing to confusion. Liar,
false egotist, who claims to love
YOU!?
I'M SICK OF SICKNESS. SICK
of hearing.

BUT WILL NOT BE DRIVEN TO MADNESS TO SACRIFICE

I hear my screaming hungers. Spit
on dreamy beauty, on gnarled
and quaint forms. Damn what dies . . .

Help me, Help me, I say in weakness.
Who can help when none are better?
When all fear to use
their eyes,
DO NOT HEAR THEIR HUNGERS

put time above
their lives,

IGNORE THE BLOOD RED BEAUTIES.

OH CHRIST LOVE GOD SHIT PAIN WHAT CAN I ASK
BUT WORK,
MOTION GESTURE WHAT BEYOND THIS BUT EARTH-DIVE
? ?
Oh sorrow that I live forever. Or
joy that I die. Each motion / make it strong /
inflexible. Psalm. Psalm. Psalm. Oh pain
of redemption. Ache.
Not redemption but liberty
enchained.

Oh dull ache of abstract meaningless. Blank
page.
HAND / / / FINGERS

YELLOW GREEN BROWN OH DEEP EYED LOVE I'VE
WALKED FROM THE ROOM
of my objects. Oh giddy blank white page. Book of my
NERVES. OH SHIT UPON
the page.
!WRITING IS LESS THAN AN ARM!
Size matters! Destroy proportion. Admit
pain. Each word is a motion of mine. Half-made,
half-felt. But real. As flames

not hard as my cock but ink
or air. Ink / Air.
REAL   !

BUILDING TO A HUGE GLORIA, ROMANTIC CRY, NEW BAROQUE SHAPE

halls of graciousness and beauty unseen before. New.
Real as plaster, fern, arm, nerve. The word nothing
but a sound of the thing felt. Abstract
or real. The grim features forcing from the snakes body
outward upward. Demands the thing new be the thing
felt. The word a sound made of the thing
felt. The control
be damned and sweet blessing to liberty.

ARM HALL

BREAK TO WHAT I AM.

!A SWEEP-STRIKE TO NEVER-BEFORE-SEEN BEAUTY!
NEVER-HEARD-OF LOVE!

To BEAUTY CONTAINING ALL! EXPLANATIONLESS!
SWEEPING HUGE TURNING
coiled bright and dim. To see all things to feel,
and stand strong in it. To straighten the synaptic
web and recirculation and stand strong in it
fresh untired and free. To see beauty,
DESTROY
what is handy, build upon it

CONTINUE
never cease. Hold head high.
Do not fear death. For
Odem there is no death
the acts are carved
eternal. Fear
only ease that is not
huge sleeping. That does
not give pleasure. Break

in each wall. Ignore re-
peats.
CARD

FORGIVE MYSELF FOR HONESTY? I ASK. I FORGIVE
and do not forgive myself for forgiveness.
OH WHAT IS THIS. WHY THIS CARE??
I RAISE MY HEAD HIGH. OH SINGING IN MY HEAD.
NO! Voice, voice I hear. Sight I see. Dream

I dream. Oh what is this?
Oh fake of honesty! Oh blood,
nerve of a star. Self-
confuser. False-vanity!

OH HAND HAND HAND HAND HAND HAND HAND HAND
HAND HAND HAND

(((To YOUR HUGE SMOOTH FACE AND HAND, BODY,
SMOOTH, IN
warm touch evening cool. I strike sick longing,
forgiving you. Wanting forgiveness. To lost
in the small words. Lost in the untensile
HEARING ANOTHER VOICE LOVE YOU
/ LOSE YOU /
Lose love the outline of my body. Lose sight
in pictures of the love I have. Oh else!
I COME! ((AWAY-DREAMING.))
And all that too incoporated. Held

IN THE BODY LIKE A NERVE
Geryon, a false beauty, fraud

HOW TO PUT IT DOWN? HOW TO CEASE??

Cease!

OH SMOKE-MAKING INTENT DREAMING OF ELSEWHERE
sick lip-service to a small shrieking voice.
Do you love me oh? As I love you?)))

OH BRAIN OH LOVE OH GOD SHIT PAIN OH HEAT
FIRE OF CONFUSIONS
I raise my head again see over the edge of
sickness. A lie. Worse than confusions. Oh parody.
Mock heroic. Tiredness. I give into love of ease.
NOT LOVE. I CANNOT THINK
I can't concentrate. Oh clear meaning
of what I feel and believe return to me.
Worse than blank pages. So little given.
Bright false images and dull
words. Till all that
comes from me is never-before-seen
beauty. Till
I no longer fight to hold vision for
an instant! And can move in it bold.
OH LONGING FOR OBJECTS. Fire of flesh
beating on the cold rocks

FUCK ODE

THE HUGE FIGURES FUCKING THE HUGE FIGURES
FUCKING THE HUGE FIGURES
FUCKING ON THE CLIFFS ON THE BANKS
IN THE BLACK RIVER
in the fields without proportion, the black clover
grown meadows. THERE IS NO SIZE! Undreaming and
vast as a dream. This is love INVENTED. The huge
COCK
slipping in the soft dream. Not dream. In the cunt,
THERE! In the mouth. The slipping of figures upon
the other. The rocking, the hugging swaying,
HOLDING.
THE FIGURES JOIN THEIR BODIES
TO THEIR BODIES,
the skin walls are joined! Arm of arm
held to arm. The huge faces and behemoth legs,
the round arms of love made anew. We slip
down into the black clover. I / slide into the
scented grass I sing in your ear. My song is nothing
but the sounds of my feeling. Music is ugly. My
song is the same as yours holding me.
ALL IS QUIET BUT MY SONG TO ME, YOUR SONG
to you. This is our touching. This
is the vast hall that we inhabit. Coiling,
standing. Cock into rose-black meat. Tongue
into rose meat. Come upon your breasts, Come
upon your tongue, come in your burrow
Cavern love snail breath strange arm line

OH SLEEP SLEEP NOT. OH STRENGTH BODY
LOVE
There are no lies in your face your eyes

I see in darkness. There is a golden
casket hanging there over our heads,
Silver, Silver Carafe, No!
!A SIGHT, SIGHT!
THE VOID OF OUR SENSES ETERNAL. THE COME! ! ! !
My cock is blue and pink in the vast
night. Night? In the vast. OH
ever undreaming I feel you / I, you
are my body as I claim it. This is not
Nothing. Oh Ever ever! ! Oh not chalice but
body. Oh tongue lined
sweetness of buttock and tight sleekness of
asshole. Oh mount of meat fur
coated, hand brushed. Huge Figures, Fucking,
perfumes eternal called perfumes. Remembrances
of this ever moment. Oh MEADOWS MEADOWS
MEADOWS MEADOWS MEADOWS MEADOWS MEADOWS
MEADOWS MEADOWS MEADOWS
MEADOWS OF THIS, tracery orange black in my closed eye touch
of clover, of all soft and destroyed body-crushed flowers
IN THE BANKS ON THE BLACK RIVERS I REPRIEVE MYSELF
from the false-to-you / myself. From the false to myself
creating moments. Each moment the last each the new
Invention. Each the last protection and attack

AND NOT THAT BUT THE BREATHING LAST.
THE HARD-ON THE FEEL-UP
The stretched cock plunging you. The Oh Not Dream, HOLDING
the grasp of myself by myself. The body known at last! ! !
!AT LAST!
YOUR HAIR IS A BLONDE FIELD
AND A MEADOW IN BLACKNESS.
THE CLOVER THE SIZE OF MY LEG! THERE IS NO SKY
eyes closed or open. Oh Love Love Already recaptured and

[227]

lost. Each instant of stone, basalt and huge each a
square boulder among the figures not lost on the eye!
THE JERT JERT JERT OF THE COME INTO THE HEAT
of my inside-cock. Burning. The tube of
myself. Oh mangled line! Oh burning beauty!
COMED EYE SOBBING AND TEARS OF LAUGHTER, OH
breathing. Oh false explanations. Freed

Of all lies the face is pure. The gestures are imm-
ortal. THE FIRE IS FIRE CONFUSIONS BURNT IN
upon themselves. What is speed? Oh false
to myself uncovered! Oh come in your pink-rose
cunt and on your tongue tip. Breast. NO! ! Shoulder
in my mouth. Bite on your buttock. Ass kissed
BEATENED AND FRESHENED   NOT LOVE NO BUT
new.
OH FEAR FEAR FEAR TORN AND GONE.
OH HUGE FIGURES, BREATH.
OH CLOVER CLOVER CLOVER AND NOT MUSIC
OH HUGE UGLINESS

that is beauty! OH beauty that is huge ugliness. Oh
vast halls of meadows and blackness. Dark
water. Oh who has been here before I
raise me in Seraph-hood! I say it risen from fear I
expand the face arm nerve muscle of myself to
include myself. The step to fill it is easy. Oh all
unsimple. Simple. Oh beatened darkness huge and whole.
MY COCK YOUR HAND OUR MOUTHS YOUR
MEAT CUNT MY SIZE

BLACK LIGHT BLACK LIGHT BLACK LIGHT BLACK LIGHT
and meat beast creatures turning huge. Light
clover cool in your hug of me of my hug.
NOT MUSIC! ! !

OH BEGONIA PETAL ON THE PAGE, Worm within.
NOT MUSIC!
My arms huge cradles on the clover. My back a block.
Your / my pant in pleasure and shriek of coming. The
waves of it and toe-twists. The muscles revolt
each seeks to become a lover. OH STOP STOP.
((Pride, liberty, love, have one meaning—Invention.))
I, my body, I, I, I, I, I, buckle!
The instant test.
NOT NOT MUSIC.
I BUCKLE FROM ONE VISION, SIGHT, FROM THE CLOVER.

((THIS IS THE CAVE OF THE VOID OF OUR SENSES.
THIS IS ALL OPEN.
Open your mouth to me You / I. Let me lay the huge
head of my cock
on your tongue again in blackness. Swell till it comes white spurts
in blackness. Let your breasts stretch as they do. What color I see
them what shape they are, solid figure. Spread your legs. The shape
you make them / I / for me I feel the hair with my tongue my
cock as I enter. Oh past, past. There is one tense. There is one.
I / HUGE FIGURE FUCKING IN BLACKNESS,
moistness of clover warm / cool. Wet of tongue and meat-cunt
cool / warm. Beige taste in blackness. As you sink to my knees
and fall to grasp you / I. Come drop on your shoulder.

THIS IS THE DARKNESS IN BLACK LIGHT THIS
IS THE CLOVER THIS
is the valley and black river. Carafe again, no
the found hunt. Not the Chase, the all moment. The whole blossom,
not the ion exchanged. The come shot and huge
slipping
BLACK WATER IN BLACKNESS WATER CASCADING
on the cliffs and the banks and the meadow.))

NO LIMIT TO THIS NO MEDALLION NO MOVED WITHIN
but all blackness and meadow, river, clover, bulks
fucking. You / I suck come from me in huge motions of mouth
blossom / cunt / arm round but. I slip down to cover
you forever. Not I outspoken but all others inspoken. Oh bright
dark I / you / I.

OH LAWRENCE, LAWRENCE, D. H. LAWRENCE, I AM WHOLE
AS IS JOHN WEBSTER,
his huge body there on the bank-tips, cliff-edge joined
his desire-love with his body. Oh see him there! ! ! ! ! ! !

WOMAN WOMAN WOMAN WOMAN WOMAN WOMAN

I—You, / I, now
FOREVER! ! !

A GARLAND

OH LET LOVE OH ME LOVE OH LET LOVE YOUR SWEET
BONES AND BREASTS
sweet slim round arms and firm ass. Touch you
where you swell. Kiss your soft flesh. Make meat
of you and bite your pale lips. Push my finger
in you, BODY, warm where. Oh let me lick. I kiss
your slim fingers. Kiss you in your hair and bite
your waist. Feel the skin of you like lace moved and
torn by the touch of what I make to you. And press
your shoulder. Hug your back
to me. And slip my dry cock under your moist ass,
and bite you on the neck. Rub your
belly with my hand and finger your lips
and hole. OH LET LOVE OH ME.
I want it.

OH LIE OH LET LOVE DOWN BEFORE ME SPREAD
YOUR HAIR LONG
on the pillow. Black pantied, no naked! Open
your eyes and mouth wide. Your dark eyes and hair
over the pillow. Leave your long white-pink open
spread before me. With a picture of Jesus beside
on the bedstead. And mouth open smile, I
climb and hunch over your face. Fondle my cock
and lick my balls beneath your chin! No
I hurry. Open your mouth wide your
red mouth, your white teeth the pink roof
of your throat. Your long hair spread
on the pillow.

OH SMIRKING SMILE OH OH MURKY HOLE BE GONE
BE LOVE

invented. Be enormous as a fuck. Fucked arm,
fucked mouth and ass. Let me lick salty
water from your belly. Let me run my stiff
cock between your breasts, beneath your arm.
I suck your tits and ears. Tongue your
clitoris. Dream and lie upon your belly, push
my fingers in your hole and feel your ass,
     and you lick and suck my
   . soft cock to make it hard again.
          !THIS IS A CLASP!
Hold my balls in your mouth and breathe
upon my ass. Lick come from my fingers. Jack
me off. Smell yourself upon my hands
and prick. I bite the arm you slip beneath
          my back.
     I plunge within the hole you open
there before me. Feel your cunt pull open
          wide.
OH SMIRKING SMILE OH OH MURKY HOLE BE GONE
          BE LOVE

OH LET OH LIE LOVE SLIP DOWN ON YOUR KNEES
          AND BLOW ME
See your mouth pushed opened spread with the size
 of the thing in it. See your lovely face mis-
shapen into new beauty. Feel the hard slick thing
     in it. Feel the pink head of it
back in your throat! Down on your knees
before me. Hands held to your cheeks and ears,
your long soft legs folded under you. Only
warm damp wet moist mouth hot hot with my cock
 in it. Working to make me come, eyes flashing
upward. Seeing the arms held to your cheeks to feel
   the cock pushing inside them. Seeing

my face above. Hearing the groan. Catching
the shot splash of come on your tongue.

LIE OH HUNCH OH LOVE CLIMB OVER ME PUT
YOUR ASS OVER
my face put your mouth over my cock. I look up
into your asshole and hole! I feel your lips and teeth
on my cock. Tongue I put against your asshole,
your sweet asscheeks I spread with my hands. Tip
tongue I move over the crease circled hole, feel
you relax and slip it inside. And feel your tense
of shame. Sleek clean inner asshole. Put my tongue
to your cunt and lick upward, the whole crease.
Tongue over hole tongue over asshole. One hand knead-
ing your breast. Feeling your hair
and breath on my toes.

ABOUT THE AUTHOR

Poet Michael McClure has also published novels, plays, and collections of essays about Nature and art. His play *The Beard* is an encounter between Billy the Kid and Jean Harlow in a blue velvet eternity. It provoked a censorship battle in Los Angeles, where the cast was arrested after each performance on nineteen consecutive nights. His deepest pursuits, aside from poetry and art, lie in biology and the edge between consciousness and physiology.

McClure's performances of poetry and his ongoing solo readings carry forward the tradition that he began with Allen Ginsberg and Gary Snyder in their first group reading at the Six Gallery in San Francisco, 1955. In recent years he has been collaborating with Ray Manzarek to bring their poetry and music to clubs and colleges; the CD of their work is titled *Love Lion*.

His numerous awards include a Guggenheim Fellowship, the Obie Award for Best Play, the Alfred Jarry Award, and a Rockefeller grant for playwriting. The National Poetry Association honored him for Distinguished Lifetime Achievement in Poetry.

McClure is featured in several films; in Scorsese's *Last Waltz* he recites Chaucer's poetry, and in Mailer's *Beyond the Law* he portrays an outlaw motorcyclist.

PENGUIN POETS